Robert Anderson

Poems on Various Subjects

Robert Anderson

Poems on Various Subjects

ISBN/EAN: 9783744716086

Printed in Europe, USA, Canada, Australia, Japan

Cover: Foto ©Andreas Hilbeck / pixelio.de

More available books at **www.hansebooks.com**

S SUBJEC[T]

BY

ANDERSON,

OF CARLISLE.

Studious of song,
...not to sing in vain.   Co...

CARLISLE,

...D BY J. MITCHELL,

FOR

THE AUTHOR,

...ARKE, New Bond-Street, L...

TO

J. C. CURWEN, ESQ. M. P.

OF WORKINGTON-HALL,

AS A TRIBUTE OF RESPECT DUE TO

HIS MANLY EEXERTIONS

IN THE CAUSE OF FREEDOM,

AND THE SPIRIT AND ZEAL

WHICH HE HAS DISPLAYED, ON ALL OCCASIONS,

IN DEFENDING THE

RIGHTS AND PRIVILEGES

OF THE

ANCIENT CITIZENS OF CARLISLE,

THESE POEMS,

(THE PRODUCTIONS OF A NATIVE)

ARE RESPECTFULLY INSCRIBED,

BY HIS MOST OBEDIENT

AND VERY HUMBLE SERVANT,

THE AUTHOR.

JUNE 18, 1798.

PREFACE.

AT this enlightened period, when Britain can boast of a COWPER, a ROSCOE, a ROGERS, a PINDAR, a HAYLEY, and a MRS. SMITH, whose works are in such high estimation, and known to every lover of Poetry, it is with the greatest diffidence the Author of the following trifles submits this volume to a numerous and respectable body of Subscribers, whose friendship has induced them to bestow on him praise for talents he cannot boast of; and on their account he ventures his feeble bark along the friendly coast, not daring, nor wishing, to launch into that dangerous sea

Where fame is seldom won—and won, soon lost.

Prevented by his humble birth from enjoying the benefits of an education which enables man-

kind to pursue the flowery path of Science, he owns with regret, that he can but peruse in his native tongue the sacred pages of the immortal few, whose works, like beacons, teach the modest Bard how to avoid the rocks of Criticism; and is conscious how much he stands beneath the notice of the literary world, well knowing that those whom he most esteems may vainly look for poetic beauties, or flights of fancy, in this volume : yet, when, like the numerous offspring of heated imaginations, it may be lost in the stream of Oblivion, he will enjoy the pleasing reflection, that not one sentence caused a blush to crimson the check of Virtue.

Having thus offered to a circle of friends the musings of hours spent in retirement (and consequently the most happy), he truts none but *the malicious will condemn an amusement so blameless, confessing, at the same time, he will be*

Proud if his artless and unpolish'd lay
Can soothe one child of Sorrow on his way.

CONTENTS.

MISCELLANIES.

PAGE.

THE Soldier, a Fragment - - - - 3
Ode to Sleep - - - - - - 8
The Peasant - - - - - - 14
Evening, a rural Fragment - - - - 16
The Slave - - - - - - - 22
Epigram - - - - - - - 24
Retirement - - - - - - - 25
The Rose - - : - - - - 28
Friendship, Love, and Wine - - - - 29
Spring, a Fragment - - - - - - 32
Ode to Content - - - - - - 50
Evening, or the Shepherds - - - - 52
Ode to Care - - - - - - - 58
Lines on visiting Corby - - - - - 60
Hymn - - - . - - - - 64
The Journey of Life : - - - - 66

EPISTLES.

1. To Robert Burns - - - - - 69
2. To a youthful Friend, with a Copy of Gregory's
   Legacy - - - - - - - 79
3. To a Friend in London - - - - 84

b

PAGE.

4. To young Lady - - - - - 89
5. To a Lady - - - - - - 93
6. To a young Lady, who requested an Epistle in
    Rhyme - - 100
7. To a young Lady, with a Copy of Relph's Poems 104
8. To a Friend, in Thanks for his Letter - - 107

SONNETS.

1. To J. C. Curwen, Esq. M. P. - - - 115
2. To the Lark - - - - - . 116
3. To an aged Parent, on seeing him shed Tears 117
4. Written in Winter - - - - - 118
5. To a Rose in Eliza's Bosom - - - 119
6. To a young Lady, with some Songs - - 120
7. Evening - - - - - - - 121
8. To John Horne Tooke, Esq. - - - 122
9. To the River Eden - - - - - 123
10. To a Redbreast - - - - - 124
11. To the same - - - - - - 125
12. To a young Lady labouring under a severe Illness 126
13. To a Poor Boy - - - - - 127
14. To Eliza - - - - - - - 128
15. To a pretended Friend - - - - 129
16. Night - - - - - - - 130
17. To the River Caldew - - - - 131
18. To Mr. Robert Carlile - - - - 132

	PAGE.
19. To Eliza - - - - - - -	133
20. Written in Spring - - - - -	134
21. To an unfortunate Female - - - -	135
22. Sonnet - - - - - - -	136

SONGS.

1. A Lassie and a Gill - - - - -	139
2. The Captive - - - - - -	142
3. Marian - - - - - - -	143
4. Generous Wine - - - - -	145
5. Ben Bowser's Maxim - - - -	147
6. Lucy Gray of Allendale - - - -	149
7. Donald of Dundee - - - - -	141
8. Poor Anna - - - - - -	153
9. Hark away - - - - - -	155
10. Dearly do I love thee - - - -	157
11. Theodore and Annette - - - -	159
12. I sigh for the Girl I adore - - - -	161
13. Luckless Jean - - - - - -	163
14. Ye who would Life's Pleasures prove - -	165
15. Polly - - - - - - -	166
16. Come, sweet Girl, and live with me - -	168
17. The Lasses o' the Lyne - - - -	170
18. Fair Sally	171
19. Eliza	173

		PAGE.
20.	Bonny Jem that's o'er the Sea	175
21.	Kate	177
22.	Absence	179
23.	Ellen and I	180
24.	Autumn	182
25.	Julia	183
26.	To-morrow	184
27.	Nanny of the Tweed	186
28.	Donald	187
29.	Willy of Eden Side	189
30.	The lovely brown Maid	191
31.	Kate of Dover	193
32.	Summer	195
33.	The sweetest Flower of Yarrow	196
34.	Go, Winds	198
35.	Honest Jack	199
36.	My Deary, O	201
37.	The Season of Love	203
38.	Collin's Complaint	204
39.	Muirland Willy	206
40.	Henry	208
41.	Dearly I love Johnny, O	210
42.	The Thrush	212
43.	The Press-Gang	214
44.	The Beggar Girl	216
45.	The Pursuit of Happiness	218
EPIGRAMS, &c.		223—227

Miscellanies.

MISCELLANIES.

THE SOLDIER,

A FRAGMENT.

Some, for hard masters, broken under arms,
In battle lopt away, with half their limbs,
Beg bitter bread thro' realms their valour sav'd.

YOUNG.

.... UNDER an aged thorn,
Whose wither'd branches Time had stripp'd of leaves,
Save just enough to shew it yet had life,
And vied with him in years, he shiv'ring stood,
Half shelter'd from the cold and beating rain;
But from keen want and all its wretchedness,
The taunt of Pride and Poverty's rude storms,
He seem'd, alas! no shelter to expect.

A crutch supported the remaining part
Of a spare body, cover'd half with weeds,

'Of coarsest texture mix'd. His shoulders bore
The patched remnant which himself had worn
Full oft on blood-stain'd fields. One piece was left,
That told the passing stranger how he stood
At the dread hour, when Carnage loud was heard,
And all around him bleeding victims lay.

As I approach'd, he bow'd; and, with a look
That seem'd to say, ' I am indeed sincere,'
A story then began, half mix'd with sighs,
That might have pierc'd a " heart flint to the core"—
For his, alas! it felt too much to feign.

When suffering Virtue craves our friendly aid,
'Tis in a tone of supplication meek,
That, in the pensive wand'rer's woe-fraught breast,
Still finds a friend, and makes the beating heart
At once dictator to the bounteous hand.

Thus in my course arrested by the tale
That's oft-times told, and told full oft in vain,

Attentive long, with silent awe, I heard,

How, in his youthful days, he vainly strove,

In filial tenderness, to heal the woes

That laid an aged parent in the dust.

Here did his sorrows seem to bleed afresh—

'Twas Nature bade his tear-swoln eyes to weep.

Then, feebly pointing to the distant hill,

He mark'd the spot where once his cottage stood,

Where he had spent life's spring, and, with the lark,

Oft hail'd the day, as forth he led his team,

With Poverty hard struggling. From the hour

Which gave him birth, he knew not Fortune's smiles,

Nor Pleasure's giddy round—the pomp of courts,

Where wild Ambition dwells; nor did he dream

That busy Care oft haunts the monarch's breast,

And Guilt attends the haughty son of pride.

Yet, tho' his flocks were few, and few his fields,

Tho' waving Plenty ne'er had crown'd his toil,

He might, with rural Innocence and Peace,

Such joys have tasted in his humble state,

As Grandeur seldom knows, had not the maid,

Whose fancied charms first fir'd his artless breast,

Whom love had call'd his own, now prov'd as false

As youthful Fancy once had thought her fair.

Despairingly he left his native meads,

The rural scene of many a youthful sport,

The seat of Industry and blooming Health,

Where his forefathers dwelt, to Pride unknown,

Won by the hero's name, discordant sounds,

And all the false appendages of war.

Now he began to tell of storming towns,

Of peaceful villages laid desolate ;

How many a merry comrade bravely fell ;

And would again have fought each battle o'er,

Calling each wound to witness what he said.

All this the poor sustainer might have sav'd,

With many a painful sigh ; for, to my ear,

Nought half so grating as the horrid tales

Of battles, sieges, and fair towns destroy'd,

With thousands falling at a tyrant's nod,

Who heeds no widow's sigh, no orphan's moan,

But glides thro' life 'twixt Luxury and Guilt.

Grown weary with his plain-told woes and sighs,

I left this houseless wand'rer ; whilst a tear,

That started at the sight of his grey hairs,

And face grief-worn, that Time had furrow'd o'er,

With half-bent body, sloping to the grave,

Told me, as on I mus'd, this son of Want

Was brother to Ambition's splendid train,

For whom he fought and bled : then did I wish,

For once, that Fortune had to me been kind ;

Then did I envy scornful Pride his wealth ;

For, to the feeling heart, what joy so great,

As when it shares a woe-worn brother's cares,

And, sympathizing, softens his distress !

O ye, who feel not Poverty's keen gripe,

But loll with Luxury on beds of down ;

While the poor warrior, on the sun-burnt heath,

Or frozen plain, in sleepless anguish lies ;

Think, think of him, the victim of your ease ;

And when he 'scapes the gore-stain'd field, where Death,

So oft a friend, the hero frees from pain,

Attentive hear the wounded wand'rer's tale,
Nor mock with scorn his honourable scars,
But let Compassion pour soft Pity's balm
Into the wounds, which only Death can cure.

ODE TO SLEEP.

Why rather, Sleep, liest thou in smoky cribs,
Upon uneasy pallets stretching thee,
And hush'd with buzzing night-flies to thy slumber,
Than in the perfum'd chambers of the great,
Under the canopies of costly state,
And lull'd with sounds of sweetest melody?

SHAKESPEARE.

HAIL, gentle soother of the human breast,
  Foe to the busy canker Care,
Whose balm can lull to rest
  The fiend Despair.

Sweet is thy draught to Mis'ry's sons, who live
   Unpitied by unfeeling Wealth;
For thou content dost give,
   And rose-cheek'd Health.

Methinks 'tis sweet, when from the sun's warm beam
   The flocks to friendly thickets fly,
By some flow'r-margin'd stream
   In peace to lie,

On thy down pillow, 'neath an old oak's shade,
   By minstrels lull'd to soft repose :
Then Memory, faithful maid,
   Forgets her woes,

And Love, with sportive Fancy, brings to view
   The faery age of gay delight,
When pleasures ever new
   Stole on the sight.

Mirth-loving Innocence enjoys thee most,
   That wanders free the brambl'd dell;
Nor can vain Grandeur boast
    Thy magic spell.

E'en now doth Fancy mark yon stately pile,
   Where high-born Pride, on ruin bent,
Enjoys frail Fortune's smile
    Without content.

How cheerless are his long enanguish'd nights,
   Stung by Reflection's keenest dart!
He knows not those delights
    That feast the heart.

Sleepless, and numb'ring the slow hours of time,
   Vain wishing for th' approach of morn,
Grief-wrung—by many a crime
    His bosom torn.

Not so the humble cottager, retir'd
From vice-engend'ring scenes of strife;
Nought envying, still admir'd,
He glides thro' life.

Methinks I see him, at the op'ning dawn,
Haste cheerful to the toil of day,
Whistling across the lawn
His cares away.

Unstain'd by crimes that haunt the seat of Pride,
Fell Discord ne'er disturbs his cot;
In peace his moments glide,
Pleas'd with his lot.

All nature owns thy animating pow'r,
That Sorrow of her sting beguiles:
Sweetner of life's sad hour,
Dear are thy smiles,

That steal from brooding Care his keenest sting,
  And check the rending pangs of love !
To thy grief-shelt'ring wing
  Oft let me rove,

When, joy-deserted, on life's dreary road,
  I sigh and think of what is past ;
For thou canst ease the load
  That's on me cast.

Oft have I woo'd thee on sad Sorrow's bed,
  When, pierc'd by man's ingratitude,
Despair, by Sadness led,
  Would fain intrude,

Telling me life was but a vale of tears,
  And happiness a fancied toy—
A scene of hopes and fears
  That knew no joy.

But, half recov'ring by thy fostering aid,
  That soothes awhile heart-probing grief,
Religion, heav'n-born maid!
  Soon gave relief.

When riot-loving Noise her levee keeps,
  Blasting what Virtue bids to bloom,
And silent Sorrow weeps
  Mid' Night's dark gloom,

O let me taste thy spirit-cheering bowl,
  Whose pow'r Lethean, grief dispels,
And charms the drooping soul
  Where Sadness dwells!

THE PEASANT.

'Tis better to be lowly born,
And range with humble livers in content,
Than to be perk'd up in a glitt'ring grief,
And wear a golden sorrow.   SHAKESPEARE.

How blest the lowly Peasant's life,
    Tho' Splendour scorns his humble lot,
Who, free from lordly cares and strife,
    Thinks no gay palace like his cot.

When Nature hails the morning grey,
    Health wakes him o'er his fields to roam;
And at the dusky close of day,
    Contentment leads him to his home. .

Brisk Labour, Mirth, and rural Sport,
    Attend him o'er his homely fare;
He knows but by its name the court,
    And wonders man should man ensnare.

With breast from pride and envy free,
  Disturbers of the tools of state,
He laughs at slaves of high degree,
  And cheerful meets the storms of fate.

Far from Riot rude and Noise,
  Far from Pleasure's magic ring,
Ever tasting life's pure joys—
  Who, ah! who, would be a king!

EVENING,

A RURAL FRAGMENT.

Hail, meek ey'd maiden, clad in sober grey,
Whose soft approach the weary woodman loves!

JOS. WARTON.

'TIS Evening mild; her fragrance scents the air;
In robe of dunness clad, she silent sits
On yon grey mountain's brow.   At her approach,
Gay Phœbus, redd'ning, gilds the placid sky,
His faint rays dancing o'er the dimpl'd stream,
Lashing his fiery coursers down the west,
As to the sloping hills, embrown'd in shade,
He bids adieu—then vanishes from man.

The cheerful cottager no longer views
His lengthen'd shadow stalk across the plain;
But, labour-wearied, marks his far-off hut,
Where Peace sits smiling at his humble gate,

And, homeward whistling, oft, with joyous gaze,
Beholds the spiky produce of his fields.

Th' exhaling flow'rs, that beam'd throughout the vale,
Diffuse no more their grateful odours round,
But, drooping, seem to mourn departing day ;
While, from their honey'd stores, th' industrious bee,
Humming her feeble flight, makes tow'rds her cell.
Returning zephyrs, from the fragrant glade,
Now sport among the willows near the stream,
Or kiss the curling surface of the deep,
From whence the twitt'ring swallow wings her way,
And, winding, steals into her clay-built nest,
To nurse her unfledg'd young till morning dawns.

No more the feather'd choir are heard around ;
All, all is silent, save the blackbird's song,
That, faintly echoing, steals along the grove,
As from the distant wood he calls his mate.
Lorn minstrel ! sweetest of the feather'd train !

c

Whose notes are welcome to the lover's ear ;
Whilst madd'ning crowds, in search of pleasure, thror
To noisy theatres, where tumult reigns,
And Folly wonders at the work of Art,
That teaches man to mimic thy sweet voice.
O I do love to hear thee, bird of spring,
When at Eve's modest hour, in peace reclin'd,
Thy wild notes linger on the passing gale !
Tho' oft hath Flora strew'd the fields with flow'rs,
And led along the meads her sportive train,
Since first, in tuneless lays, I vainly strove,
In pensive mood, on the blithe-warbling flute,
To cheat awhile the busy canker Care ;
Yet, list'ning to thy plaintive melody,
I sighing say, my time hath been misspent !

Cherish'd by Hope, the lover fondly waits,
In anxious anguish, at th' appointed shade.
A thousand doubts disturb his artless breast,
And oft he gazes for the promis'd maid.

Upon the green, the shepherd's rural pipe
Proclaims to distant meads the lively dance,
And calls the younker to the festive ring,
Where Mirth and frolic Joy light-footed stray,
And sportive Gladness mocks the toils of day :
The village train now mingling in the throng
With sprightly glee. E'en Age forgets his pain,
And joins the cheering song, or harmless joke,
Recounting strange the tales of former days;
What wonders he atchiev'd to gain the fair,
And bore away the prize: then blooming health
Glow'd on his cheeks, now furrow'd o'er by time.
The rustics round in mute attention stand,
List'ning with wistful gaze to the village sage.
Full oft the laugh of innocence goes round,
And many a sigh steals forth at artless tales
In praise of virtue, till the darkning hours
Invite the happy few to soft repose.

Evening, I hail thy hours of gay content,
That to this pensive bosom still are dear!
Tho' I no more across the mist-clad hill
Steal forth with sighs to meet my soul's true-love;
Yet oft, by Fancy led, my vagrant feet
Bend tow'rds the woods, or cowslip-painted meads,
To trace the scene of many a youthful sport;
And, nurs'd by Solitude, awhile from care,
Fond Memory glances at the joys that were.
'Tis then great Nature charms the wand'ring eye,
Whose scenes luxuriant give the soul delight;
'Tis then, hid from the world, man tastes of bliss
That Reason and Religion most approve.

When in Retirement's shade, pleas'd I behold
The enlivening orb of day dart his mild beams
Aslaunt the upland lawn, or hanging wood,
Or tinge with partial gleam some distant tow'r:
Calm Contemplation steals upon my mind;
Then turning to that Pow'r who rules on high
A thought-entranced wight, thus I exclaim—

Alas ! this life's a transient summer day,
And man, frail insect ! sports away his morn,
(A child of Folly caught in Pleasure's snare)
Nor thinks the present hour may be his last !
Then keen Reflection points to age, life's eve,
And whispers, like a flow'r upon the plain
My tott'ring head must bend, as feebly on
Tow'rds home I wander thro' this rugged path,
Till Death shall close in sleep my wearied eyes.

THE SLAVE.

TORN from every dear connection,
  Forc'd across the yielding wave,
The Negro, stung by keen reflection,
  May exclaim, Man's but a Slave !

In youth, gay Hope delusive fools him,
  Proud her vot'ry to deprave ;
In age, self-interest over-rules him—
  Still he bends a willing Slave.

The haughty monarch, fearing REASON
  May her sons from ruin save,
Of traitors dreaming, plots and treason,
  Reigns at best a sceptr'd Slave.

His minion, Honesty would barter,
  And become Corruption's knave ;
Won by *ribband*, *star*, or *garter*,
  Proves himself Ambition's Slave.

Yon Patriot boasts a pure intention,
And of RIGHTS will loudly rave,
Till silenc'd by a *place* or *pension*,
Th' apostate sits a courtly Slave.

In pulpit perch'd, the pious preacher
Talks of conscience wond'rous grave ;
Yet not content, the *tithe-paid teacher*
Pants to loll a mitr'd Slave.

The soldier, lur'd by sounds of glory,
Longs to shine a hero brave ;
And, proud to live in future story,
Yields his life—to Fame a Slave.

Mark yon *poor* miser o'er his treasure,
Who to Want a mite ne'er gave ;
He, shut out from peace and pleasure,
- Starves—to Avarice a Slave.

The lover to his mistress bending,
    Pants, nor dares her hand to crave ;
Vainly sighing, time misspending—
    Wisdom scorns the fetter'd Slave.

Thus dup'd by Fancy, Pride, or Folly,
    Ne'er content with what we have ;
Toss'd 'twixt Hope and Melancholy,
    Death at last sets free the Slave.

EPIGRAM.

SAYS Dick, what makes each tyrant dread
    That simple word nam'd REASON ?—
Reason's the friend of TRUTH, cries Ned,
    And Truth too oft is Treason.

RETIREMENT.

An humble roof, plain bed, and humble board,
More clear and more untainted sweets afford,
Than all the tumult of vain greatness brings
To kings, or the swoln favourites of kings.

CREECH.

NEAR a murmuring rill, in a cottage of thatch,
From the haunts of the great I'd reside,
Where the giant Ambition should ne'er lift my latch,
Nor my garden or grove strike the eye of gay Pride.

Undisturb'd by the riot or noise of the town,
In Retirement my moments I'd spend,
Alike to pert Folly and Slander unknown ;
The rich I'd not envy, give me but a friend,

Whose converse, still pleasing, and counsels sincere,
From my bosom would banish dull Care ;

Who, if Grief e'er assail'd me, would drop the soft tear,
And, if Poverty frown'd, still his all I might share.

If Memory glanc'd at the follies of youth,
When Pleasure my feet did betray,
Calm Reflection would teach me the lesson of truth,
And warn to look forward to life's closing day.

With joy would I welcome the verdure of spring,
When gazing at eve o'er the plain ;
Or join with my Emma the heart-cheering ring,
Far, far from keen Slander and all her dull train.

In summer, awak'd by the heralds of morn,
From care-killing revels still free,
We'd taste the pure breeze on the hill or the lawn,
Where Health, blooming Health, holds her sportive
levee.

Oft at noon-tide, eváding the sun's fervid glow,
We'd hie to Seclusion's cool bow'r,

And weep o'er her* verse, forc'd by Sorrow to flow ;

Or, musing with Cowper, from Care steal an hour.

Tho' few mark the wants of the helpless and poor,

Whom the cold hand of Misery deforms ;

Tho' few heed the pangs they are doom'd to endure,

Or shield the weak wand'rers from Want's bitter

storms ;

Should the child of Misfortune ask alms at my gate,

I'd turn not in scorn from his woe,

But attentively hear him his suff'rings relate,

While my Emma her bounty should freely bestow. ·

Thus a friend to mankind would I journey thro' life,

Nor at Fate's various trials repine ;

But contended, and free from Ambition and Strife,

At Death's awful summons I'd cheerful resign.

* Mrs. Smith.

D 2

THE ROSE.

A ROSE I mark'd the other day,
  The garden's gayest pride ;
And as it hasten'd to decay,
  To Emma thus I cried ;

‘ Behold, sweet maid, that dying flow'r,
  ‘ Which late perfum'd the air :
‘ It bloom'd—it wither'd in an hour—
  ‘ Just emblem of the fair !

‘ In life's gay summer, Beauty's charms
  ‘ Awhile may give delight ;
‘ But soon Misfortune's bitter storms
  ‘ The blooming bud may blight.

‘ Struck by the conq'ring hand of Time,
  ‘ Thus youth with beauty flies :
‘ Then, O sweet flow'ret, in thy prime,
  ‘ The present moment prize !’

FRIENDSHIP, LOVE, AND WINE.

YE pow'rs, thro' life may this be mine,
To taste pure Friendship, Love, and Wine,
In some lone nook where Quiet dwells—
Quiet, that heeds not Folly's bells,
But laughs at Grandeur, Wealth, and Fame,
And Envy knows but by its name.
Safe from Ambition's madd'ning glare,
I with my friend each comfort share,
And chase away the canker Care ;
Whilst Emma's grace and matchless smile,
The lazy hours doth oft beguile :
Then mellow'd by the sparkling bowl,
Content I mark the seasons roll,
And with good-humour cheerful sing,
Nor heed pale Sorrow's baneful sting.

Let heroes seek the carnag'd field,
For fancied fame their life to yield ;

Let thoughtless lordlings seek the court,

Where Slander, Pride, and Vice resort;

Let patriots for their country rail,

And banish'd Freedom's loss bewail;

Let sons of Commerce plow the main,

Each fancied gem for fools to gain;

Let greedy misers toil for wealth,

And blast the roseate charms of health;

Still busy, busy they may be,

Whilst I am easy, happy, free.

Free from all jealousies and fears,

Shall I make life a vale of tears,

And pine for what would cares increase?

No—let me live with humble Peace;

And, whilst I ride the stormy sea,

Heed not the slaves of high degree,

But do my duty merrily,

And taste of pleasure in my prime,

Nor mind the meddling grey-beard Time.

Tho' oft he whispers, man grows old,

In spite of fame, in spite of gold,

And tells me life is but a day,

Till forc'd to join my kindred clay,

I'll laugh and quaff the hours away ;

For I with Care have nought to do—

Ye sons of wealth, he dwells with you !

And why should man for riches pine,

When blest with Friendship, Love, and Wine.

SPRING,

A FRAGMENT.

A thing of shreds and patches.   SHAKESPEARE.

THE snow's dissolv'd, the chilly winter's fled,
And all its gloomy hurricanes o'erpast.
Now blooming SPRING, in greenest mantle dress'd,
Adorn'd with flow'rets wild of various hues,
Comes smiling forth, borne on th' expanded wings
Of zephyrs sweet, attended by her train,
Gay Laughter, frolic Joy, and sprightly Mirth.
At her approach, what raptures swell the breast;
The rivers, bound no longer by the chain
Of hoary winter, murm'ring soothe the ear.
Nature, recov'ring from her languid state,
Rejoices at the change, and welcomes Spring.

Behold th' ascending sun, his feeble rays
Scarce piercing thro' the misty atmosphere;

Yet his gteat influence and genial warmth
Call vegetation forth. See all around
The flow'rs impatient to disclose their bloom,
Their honey'd stores just op'ning on the sight,
To welcome animating Spring's return.
The snow-drop, earliest of the feeble few,
Shoots boldly forth ere Winter's rage is spent,
Emblem of Innocence, with down-cast head,
Asham'd to shew its beauty to the world.
How different seems the tulip, gaudy flow'r !
How gaily deck'd, yet priz'd but for its shew !
So shines the witless beau—vain, tinsell'd thing !—
That glides thro' life unnotic'd but for dress.
The humble violet, like modest Worth,
So oft unheeded, with the primrose dwells,
'Mid brambl'd glades, or on the moss-grown bank,
Meek pair ! thus Virtue often lives retir'd,
Unknown to Fashion, or her glitt'ring train,
And droops unseen far from Life's busy crowd !
With odorif'rous breath, the lily pale

E

Seems fairer than Melissa's snowy breast;
While the gay rose, full swelling in the bud,
Pride of the garden, opes its vernal sweets,
And mocks the town-bred lady's boasted charms.
Ye fair, who proudly shine in borrow'd dyes,
Still scorning artless Modesty, whose bloom
Denotes fresh health, and far outvies the rouge,
Why vainly strive to rival this gay flow'r?—
Your artful fragrance ne'er can be compar'd
With the exhaling sweetness of the rose.
Since life is chequer'd by a thousand ills,
That Fate hath wisely order'd man to bear,
And beauty is at best a gilded toy,
A glitt'ring bauble, plaything of an hour,
That oft unthinking Folly doth ensnare,
Happiest is he who, led by mental charms,
That cheer the mind, e'en 'midst Misfortune's gloom,
Nor fade but in the wintry arms of Death.
Since then 'tis vain to prize what soon decays,
Let each weak flow'r that decks the gay parterre,

Or sheds around its odours on the plain,

An useful lesson to frail man impart,

And seem a little moralizing friend.

How oft we see them nipp'd by piercing frosts,

Or blasted in the bud.   Just so it fares

With Virtue, whom the wintry storms of Vice

Too oft assail, and crush before it blooms.

Like flow'rs, we shoot in youth, life's budding spring;

Like them we bend beneath the storms of Fate,

And fall at age, life's winter's keen approach.

Now, by the vivifying heat of Spring,

The twitt'ring swallow from her torpor wakes;

Rejoic'd she skims the surface of the deep,

And oft disturbs the angler by the stream,

Telling the joy she feels to all around.

Arise, she cries, behold gay Spring is come !

Ye swains, brisk Labour calls you to the fields ;

Health, rose-cheek'd Health, invites you to her bow'r,

And spreads for you her floral carpet round.

Ye cheerful songsters of the woods, awake,
And greet gay Spring, in liveliest verdure deck'd ;
Let woods and groves seem vocal with your lays,
Singing the beauties of the smiling year.

Sweet season ! welcome to yon sportive train
Of younkers, who attend the village school.
Methinks I see them, at the well-known hour,
When Eve's approach lulls ev'ry care to rest,
No longer forc'd to dread the haughty frown,
The look pedantic, or the stern command,
Of him who much doth boast, yet never sought
The sullen village wonder, Wisdom's path,
Nor trod the maze of Science, proud to reign
A self-taught despot o'er a feeble few,
Who, from the shackles of confinement freed,
Like prisoners 'scaping from a dungeon's gloom,
With Liberty o'erjoy'd, they revel round,
And shew to man how soon the youthful mind
Pants to throw off restraint.—O LIBERTY !

Dear art thou to mankind, celestial maid!

Whose name the boastful hireling hears appall'd;

I do adore thee, wand'rer tho' thou art!

Too little known—and known, too little priz'd.

Thou light refulgent, that canst ever cheer

The lowly traveller on his lonely way

O'er life's dull path—sweet goddess, hear my pray'r,

And deign to visit oft my humble cell!

Grant me thy smiles, I ask not pow'r or wealth—

Pow'r that blind Fortune oft to th' worthless gives,

To rob e'en Misery of her hard-earn'd store.

Aye in thy train dwells laughter-loving Health;

And she, coy maid, who loves the hill and dale,

Straying with Innocence the russet meads,

Far from the dazzling splendour of the court—

She whom the artless shepherds name Content,

Whose smile no tyrant's ill-gain'd wealth can buy,

Dread of Ambition wild and pamper'd Pride,

Rapacious rulers of the blood-stain'd earth,

Who break the strongest link of Nature's chain,

And make e'en murder pleasure—war a trade;

At whose command pale Famine stalks around,

And thousands drink the bitter cup of woe.

Without thee, life moves slow from day to day;

And man, the cheerless pilgrim, sorrowing bends

Beneath his burden painful, journeying on

His threescore years of sadness; and at length

Bids welcome to the friendly stroke of Death.

E'en such were Gallia's sons, degenerate race!

Who bow'd supinely to licentious sway;

Of Britons and their neighb'ring states the scorn.

I am a Briton, and I love to hear

Of nations struggling in the cause of truth,

Tearing Corruption from her baseless seat,

To gain for man what Reason calls his own.

E'en so did Frenchmen, envy of the world,

In arts unrivall'd as in arms renown'd.

Rous'd by thy presence, how the noble mind

Contemns the fetters that would man enslave;

And as the stars evanish from the light,

So Superstition and Oppression base
Their influence yield when LIBERTY appears.

Again fond Fancy marks the village band,
And Retrospection lingers with delight
On hours " ere Sorrow had proclaim'd me man."
Their's is life's spring: no brooding cares intrude;
No sorrows damp the moments due to sport.
Some rig the feeble bark with nautic pride,
And, anxious, see it by the gale o'erset,
Like the vain youth who boldly ventures down
The dang'rous stream of Pleasure.   Others rove
With eager haste across far distant meads,
Thro' briary copse, or thick entangl'd wood,
Watching each passing day, with prying care,
The half-fledg'd brood of linnet, lark, or thrush;
Or boldly clamb'ring up the branching pine,
To rob the stock-dove of her tender charge.
O Cruelty! thou baneful foe to youth!
Seizing his mind ere Virtue guides his steps,

At once thy willing votary he submits,

And lordly man, pride of his Maker's works,

Becomes a very tyrant in his sphere.

Ah, age of bliss! how oft, with dire regret,

Must painful Memory weep at pleasures past;

How oft recal the hours of life's fair morn,

Scenes of fond youth, that like the seasons change;

But change not, like the seasons, to return!

Then infant Fancy, by false Hope beguil'd,

Unnumber'd joys so wantonly pourtray'd.

Sweet was the prospect, and I lov'd to trace

And dwell on scenes of perfect happiness.

Delusive dream, that once could lull to rest

Each little care this artless bosom knew,

Ere I had ventur'd on life's billowy sea,

Ere I had learn'd to brave the storms of Fate,

Th' ungrateful taunt that mocks another's woe,

Or guard against the world and all its snares!

Thus, when the mariner affrighted hears

The awful murmurs of th' impendent storm,

Of ireful tempest, and the lightning's glare,
Awhile forgetful, e'en at Death's approach,
Fond Fancy wafts him to his native shore,
And paints some dear lov'd image to his sight :
A mistress fair, who weeps, but vainly weeps ;
A faithful friend, who hopes his safe return :
Pleasures remember'd steal upon his mind,
And force for what is past the painful sigh.
Again he clings to Hope, whose cheering ray
The fainting mind lights to its wish'd-for haven.

Each hedge and coppice now seem clad in green,
And every tree in opening foliage stands.
How chang'd the forest, and what various hues
Arrest the wond'ring eye ; whilst to the ear
The song of cheerful Labour and the stroke
Of woodman distant sound along the dell.
Again the stately oak puts forth its leaves,
Whose stem so late was clad with crusted snow,
Forming the shade of many a rural sport,

F

The harmless gambol, or the sprightly dance,
That cheers the rustic when his labour's o'er,
And makes industry seem a pleasing toil.
Hither the pensive village youth repairs,
When roscid Evening steals along the plain,
And, whisp'ring, tells of innocence and love
Tales artless as the blushing maid he woos.

How sweet the concert heard from spray to spray,
In notes melodious; whilst along the woods
Echo returns the heart-enliv'ning lays.
No music soothes like yours the listning ear,
Ye minstrels gay, whose care-beguiling songs
So oft arrest the wearied traveller's feet;
Whose harmony wild-warbling hails the morn,
And plaintive orisons mourn close of day.
Sweeter the matin of the soaring lark,
The mellow blackbird's evening call of love,
Or philomela's dirge, when all is hush'd,
Than the fam'd organ's hoarsely-swelling note,

Or labour'd concert, clamorously loud.

When Folly's sons are reeling home to rest,

And sleepless anguish shrinks at day's broad glare,

Oft let me trace the dewy meads, to hear

The woodland choir give welcome to the sun,

And bid the shepherd quit his humble bed

To tend his fleecy care. Ah, happy state!

Far from each vice that haunts the polish'd town!

Tho' shut in lowly hut by Winter's breath,

Pensive he thro' his tatter'd casement views

The pendent icicles hang from his roof,

The dreary prospect of his whiten'd fields,

The frowning mountains and the leafless trees,

Or hears the wind hoarse murm'ring thro' the vale,

Whirling the flaky snow in furious blasts,

Yet say, ye **gay** deck'd sons of Pride and Wealth,

Ye vaunting nothings of life's summer day,

Who heed not struggling Merit's modest pray'r,

Merit that, unprotected, blooms and dies;

Who spurn at humble Poverty's hard fare,

And think that Honesty is but a name;

Say what true joys doth life to you afford?

Alas! tho' pamp'ring Lux'ry on you waits,

'Tis but too oft a daily scene of vice:

Heedless you hurry on a short career

Down the steep precipice that leads to ruin,

Not daring to reflect on what is past.

How strange that man should careless risk his all,

Both in this world and that which is to come,

For a self-fancied shadow fools call Pleasure!

Just view the peaceful shepherd on the plain;

See ruddy health adorn his cheerful face;

Hear him contented tune his past'ral pipe,

Or sing his artless ditties of fond love;

Then say, can all the grandeur of the east,

For which e'en monarchs wade thro' seas of blood,

And sink in desolation peopled states,

Buy half the happiness he still enjoys?

Few cares his tranquil bosom e'er invade;

Contentment, sweet companion, cheers his days,

And Peace his humble pillow guards by night.

No guilty pangs disturb his noon-tide rest,

When stretch'd beneath the hawthorn shade* he lies,

Unknown to him is Vice, accurs'd lamia,

That, cover'd by weak Fashion's gaudy mask,

Lures the unwary wand'rer from his path !

His dog the constant comrade of each hour :

Fond, faithful animal ! how much unlike

Deceitful man, who boasts of Reason's laws,

Yet offers friendship only to betray !

The artless shepherd, far from Pride's gay seat,

Industrious follows Virtue's golden rule ;

And, cheer'd by meek Religion's brightning rays,

Still scorns whate'er he thinks degrades his name.

---

* Gives not the hawthorn-bush a sweeter shade
To shepherds looking on their silly sheep,
Than doth a rich embroider'd canopy
To kings who fear their subjects' treachery ?
O, yes, it doth, a thousand fold it doth.
                              SHAKESPEARE.

Transported now the pencill'd artist sees

The landscape smile around. Each forest scene

Wears a new robe that youthful fancy aids,

Transported now Orlando loves to roam,

What time the sun, with animating glow,

Steals down the saffron'd west, his fainting rays

Cheq'ring with various tints the sloping wood ;

Led by the murm'ring of the gilded stream

To seek the grove thick shaded o'er with trees,

The moss-grown bank, or unfrequented glade,

Where, far from riot or tumultuous noise,

He follows Nature in her wildest haunts ;

She who first taught him, with a mother's care,

To taste of joys that never fail to please ;

She who first taught his infant steps to bend

Tow'rds Wisdom's flow'ry, unfrequented path,

Where all is sweet retirement, peace, and love.

Inspir'd by her, he copies oft the scene

Where beauties picturesque can charm the mind ;

Inspir'd by her, he sings fair Virtue's praise

In numbers tuneful, or the pow'r of love,
And woos with her the wood-nymph Solitude.

Now the expanding mind, that, like a flow'r
Half open'd by the cheering rays of spring,
Tires with the fancied pleasures of the town,
Where Virtue, timid as the harmless hare,
Is close pursu'd by Slander's yelping pack ;
Where haggard Vice reigns with despotic sway,
Fell Envy, Pride, and Folly in her train.
The calm contemplatist still loves to dwell
Secluded from the town's mistaken joys,
And seeks Contentment in the rural shade,
Where Nature smiles around in varied hues ;
For what can more delight the busy eye,
Or fill with greater joy the anxious mind,
Than to behold the landscape spread around,
In liveliest colours dress'd—vast sight sublime !
The sloping hills by tow'ring trees o'erarch'd ;
The verdant meads with gayest flow'rs bedeck'd ;

The fields of rising grain, transporting sight !

When waving by the Evening's gentle breeze—

A plenteous prospect for the ploughman's toil.

What are th' encircling columns, splendid domes,

Of glitt'ring palaces, or halls of state,

The costly mansion, the gay lordling's pride,

The labour'd grottos, or the mazy walks

Of gardens tame, dispos'd by feeble Art,

Where man, presumptuous, Nature would excel !

Compare them with the peasant's ivy'd cot,

But form'd a friendly shelter to afford

From beating rains and Winter's piercing breath.

Tho' haughty Grandeur scorns his humble roof,

And wond'ring Folly flies from Virtue's seat,

Yet honest Industry calls him her own ;

And, Grandeur, Folly, and Ambition, know,

'Tis by his hardy toil and sweating brow

That you support a life of affluence,

Of luxury, and self-devouring Sloth.

Tho' for his board the clust'ring grape ne'er yields

Its juice luxurious ; yet his cattle give
The wholesome, boasted beverage of man,
Priz'd ere the cultur'd vine had pow'r to steal
From him his reason.   Tho' before his gate
No artful fountains, deck'd with sculptur'd nymphs,
Afford him water ; still the neighb'ring springs
Salute his ear, as from the rugged clifts,
Or summits of the rocks, they murm'ring fall
In loud cascades : he sees them rivulets form,
Laving their osier'd banks from steep to steep,
In soft meanders gliding thro' the vale :—
Nature, great mistress, forms the peasant's walks,
His groves umbrageous, and his cool retreats,
'That Art presumes in vain to imitate.

ODE TO CONTENT.

CONTENT, thou mild and cheerful guest,
Gay sunshine of the human breast,
Why dost thou fly this humble shed,
And leave me mourning pleasures fled?
When Youth enjoy'd his faery reign,
And Sorrow trac'd my steps in vain,
Then I life's glitt'ring prospect view'd,
And Virtue sought among the crowd,
Nor dreamt that she, coy maid, would dwell
In cottage lowly near the silent dell.

Companion of life's joyous hours,
With thee I sought the peaceful bowers;
When Summer bade her flow'rets bloom,
And hawthorns lent a rich perfume:
On Eden's mazy banks we stray'd,
And Nature's various scenes survey'd;

The scatter'd hamlets, winding vales;
The straying flocks, the verdant dales;
The lucid stream that roll'd along
Responsive to the blackbird's evening song:

But now the sportive hours are flown,
And I no more thy influence own;
The prospects that could once delight
Have vanish'd from my longing sight,
And left me wand'ring 'mid the storm,
My course scarce able to perform.
Ah, life of life! thy loss I mourn,
But dare not hope thy sweet return;
For oft Reflection tells this truth,
That gay CONTENT is but the friend of youth.

EVENING,

OR

THE SHEPHERDS.

THE village bell proclaim'd to Labour rest ;
The parting sun reel'd down the saffron'd west;
His mild rays gleaming softly ting'd the wood,
And lightly sported with the silver flood ;
Hush'd was the grove that late was heard so gay,
Save from the brake the blackbird's evening lay ;
All, all was silent in the winding vale,
Save Eden's murmurs borne along the gale ;
When, on a moss-clad bank with poplars crown'd,
Where the pale primrose shed its sweets around,
Love led two youthful shepherds to the shade,
And listning Echo heard the plaints they made.

COLLIN.

Behind yon hill, where stands the aged oak
That seems to scorn the hardy woodman's stroke ;

Where the pure streamlet gurgles thro' the dell,

And Peace, Content, and Innocence do dwell;

Where oft at dawn, beneath the willow-tree,

Health, roseate Health, convenes her gay levee;

From Riot safe, and all the false-nam'd joys

Of Vice, that timid Virtue oft destroys,

There Anna blooms, fair as th' half-open'd flow'r

That yields its fragrance from the thick-wov'n bow'r.

EDWY.

Yon distant pines that meet my tear-dimm'd eyes,

Above whose tops the smoky columns rise,

Shield a lone cottage from the bitter north—

There dwells my Emma, artless maid of worth,

Fairer than fairest blossoms on the thorn;

Sweet as the light-wing'd zephyrs of the morn.

E'en now methinks I hear her in the vale

Sing blithe, as homeward tripping with her pail;

And, ah! who knows but some lov'd, happier youth

Hears Emma's vows, nor doubts her love and truth.

COLLIN.

Long ere this bosom felt the pangs of love,
With Anna oft I saunter'd in the grove,
Or pluck'd the fairest wild flow'rs on the heath,
Proud if for her I form'd the gayest wreath.
In spring the linnet's tender brood we sought,
And heard with pleasure each wild warbler's note.
Ah, happy hours ! when nought but joy we knew,
And Hope still promis'd what fond Fancy drew !

EDWY.

Full sixteen summers, Collin, have I seen,
And few like me could foot it on the green ;
But now of peace bereft by Emma's eyes,
No more the sprightly village dance I prize.
Tho' shepherds all admir'd my artless lays,
That ne'er were tun'd but in my fair one's praise,
The pipe which oft beguil'd the tedious night
Is broke ; for music now yields no delight,
Since Emma, heedless of the pensive strain,
Laughs at his love, nor pities Edwy's pain.

COLLIN.

Tho' few the acres, Edwy, I can boast,
And by the murrain half my kine were lost;
Tho' Wealth may scorn and fly my humble cot;
Yet Wealth the peaceful shepherd envies not:
All, all I ask'd my Anna's smile could give—
With her 'twere happiness on earth to live;
But, from her, life seems fraught with every care,
For absence only adds to keen despair.
Still active Fancy fondly loves to trace
Her charms attractive and her matchless face.
Sweet to the lark the first appraoch of morn;
Sweet to the ploughman fields of rising corn;
Sweet is the woodbine to th' industrious bee;
But sweeter far is Anna's smile to me.

EDWY.

As late upon yon osier'd bank I stood,
My image viewing in the chrystal flood,
Alas! I cried, can Emma prove untrue!
Then sighing bade the weary world adieu.

But Reason soon assum'd her wonted sway,

And from the dang'rous brink I turn'd away,

Vowing no more to think of Emma's charms—

Still tyrant Love this panting bosom warms.

Tho' oft I strive to triumph o'er my pain,

Soon, soon, alas! the smart returns again.

COLLIN.

A lambkin late, the fav'rite of my fair,

Ah, envied lot! my Anna's constant care,

As browsing where yon oak nods o'er the steep,

Fell from the precipice into the deep;

Sudden I plung'd amid the chrystal tide,

And with her tender youngling gain'd the side:

Rejoic'd the trembling wand'rer she caress'd,

While I, unheeded, many a sigh repress'd.

EDWY.

In vain I seek my Emma in the bower,

Where oft was spent the happy noon-tide hour;

Each woodbine seems with me to droop its head,
And say, the sportive hours of love are fled;
Silence now reigns where Mirth once lov'd to dwell,
And each carv'd tree some faithless vow doth tell:
Oft on her much-lov'd name I fondly gaze—
Ah! rude memorial of life's joyous days!

COLLIN.

In vain around me cheerful linnets sing;
Unheeded now the blooming flow'rets spring:
To the dark dell in pensive mood I fly,
Where nought but Echo hears my rending sigh.
Ah! soon some bard, whose strains can well impart
A tale of sadness to the lover's heart,
Shall weep to tell the cause of Collin's woe,
As pointing to the stone where I'm laid low.

EDWY.

Night bids us quick depart, my mournful friend,
For all around her chilling dews descend:

H

Soon as bright Sol to-morrow's course hath run,

And Evening tells the swain his task is done,

Let's hither fly—but now, spite of our woes,

Seek—what the love-lorn shepherd seldom knows.

ODE TO CARE.

WHY, Care, art thou still hov'ring here,
Thou keen disturber of my breast,
Whose cot Ambition comes not near,
Nor gay-deck'd Pride, that haughty guest?
Life would be life, were't not for thee—
Begone, tormentor, far from me!

Go visit wild Ambition's court,
Where man is basely bought and sold;
Or to the miser's hut resort,
And mark him bending o'er his gold;
Or seek yon stately marbl'd hall,
Where thoughtless Pleasure holds her ball.

I envy not the great their wealth,
  Nor will I bow to Fashion's slave ;
Friendship, Freedom, Peace, and Health—
  These, these awhile are all I crave :
And but for thee, thou canker Care,
These choicest blessings might I share.

LINES

UPON VISITING CORBY,

THE SEAT OF

HENRY HOWARD, ESQ.

The pleasant seat, the ruin'd tow'r,
The naked rock, the shady bow'r ;
The town and village, dome and farm ;
Each give each a double charm,
Like pearls upon an Ethiop's arm.

DYER.

Y E few who court the sylvan shade,

The moss-clad hill, the deep cascade ;

The hanging wood, enamell'd grove,

The hollow rock, sweet scene of love !

Where Echo many a sighing tale

Bears soft upon the balmy gale ;

To you I give the artless lay,

Who Nature's wildness pleas'd survey.

Around the birds are heard to sing;
Around the flow'rs are seen to spring,
Whose sweets the ambient air perfume,
And each its neighbour mocks in bloom.
Its blossoms fair the hedge-row bears;
Its countless shades the forest wears.
The ivy'd oaks their branches spread;
The fragrant woodbine hangs its head,
Creeping around the rude-wov'n bow'r,
Or near the time-rent mould'ring tow'r.
How gay appears each distant scene,
Where scatter'd hamlets intervene;
And winding vales and verdant hills
The pensive breast with transport fills.
Here rev'ling Mab, the faery queen,
By wond'ring villagers is seen,
In harmless gambols on the green,
Attended by her sportive train,
When Cynthia gilds the dewy plain;
Or tripping round the spangl'd thorn,
Till banish'd by th' approach of morn.

Here bubbling springs, in sadd'ning sound,
Steal o'er the bank with poplars crown'd,
Where silver Eden glides along,
Responsive to the woodlark's song ;
And, near the rugged rocky steep,
The Naiads sport upon the deep ;
While on the shore, with watchful eye,
Attentive to his well-shap'd fly,
The angler snares the silv'ry fry.

Tho' some pursue the pomp of courts,
Or seek delusive Pleasure's sports :
In wand'ring o'er her mazy round,
Content, alas! is seldom found ;
But oft her paths the feet betray
That venture on her thorny way,
And man too late perceives the snare,
When fall'n a prey to cank'ring Care.
Here, free from busy scenes of srife,
True joys attend the rural life.

Then ye who would these pleasures share,
To CORBY's lone retreats repair,
For Peace and Virtue wait you there.

Let others praise the LEASOWES' plains,
Where SHENSTONE tun'd his love-lorn strains—
Strains to the pensive bosom dear,
That claim the tribute of a tear :—
Yet, tho' he sung of groves and bow'rs ;
Of winding paths bestrewn with flow'rs ;
Of murm'ring streamlets, echoing glades,
Woods, lawns, and minstrel-haunted shades ;
His lambkins sporting near the brook,
His garland, pipe, or shepherd's crook ;
'Twas Art and Fancy brought to view,
What Nature here presents to you.

HYMN,

WRITTEN SÚNDAY, FEBRUARY 11, 1798.

—————

To thee what praises can I give,
Thou great Creator, Lord of all,
Whose goodness 'tis that man shall live,
Whose will it is that man shall fall.

Around where'er I cast mine eyes,
They pleas'd behold thy works divine;
My daily wants thy hand supplies—
Then, O! what praises, Lord, are thine,

Whose heav'nly light the soul can cheer,
When earthly sorrows on me press;
Whose voice is to the sinner dear,
And makes his pond'rous load seem less.

Since life, O Lord, is but a span,
And soon we mingle with the dust;
Since thine's the power, how blest is man
Who in such goodness puts his trust.

Why doth weak mortals weep at fate,
Why murmur at thy holy will;
'Thy servant, whatsoe'er my state,
Teach me to be contented still.

Keep me from Vice and all her train,
Who seem forgetful of thy word;
Keep me from Pride and Grandeur vain,
And may each hour be thine, O Lord.

Forgive me if I chance to stray,
And let me to thy path return;
There guide me in thy holy way,
Till life's short taper cease to burn.

THE JOURNEY OF LIFE.

As we journey thro' life, often tost to and fro,
Nurs'd by Hope, at each phantom we catch as we go,
And the prospects around us enraptur'd we view,
Till they vanish, as shrinks from the sun-beams the dew:
On the soft lap of Pleasure awhile we are borne;
Yet, in seizing the rose, are oft pierc'd by its thorn.
Ah! how thoughtless is man, who pursues a false glare,
That soon hastens his ruin, or adds to his care,
When RELIGION alone can life's sorrows remove,
And lead to the mansion of Pleasure above.

Epistles.

EPISTLES.

TO ROBERT BURNS.

~~~~

WRITTEN AND SENT TO THAT CELEBRATED SCOTTISH
BARD A FEW WEEKS BEFORE HIS DEATH.

Nay, do not think I flatter;
For what advancement may I hope from thee,
That no revenue hast, but thy good spirits,
To feed and clothe thee?   SHAKESPEARE,

SIN' sense and reason baith unite
In ye, to gi'e mankind delight,
Forgi' me gin I bauldly write
            In lowly strain :
O man, could I like ye indite,
            'Twould mak' me fain !

Thought I, I'se try my pen at rhyme,
Gif I can hit o' words to chyme;
Sin poetizin is nae crime,   ·
           I'll do my best: .
In cam' the Muse—'twas just in time—
           To do the rest.

In naming BURNS, I saw her smile;
Says she, ' I've known him a lang while,
' And ane sae free frae artfu' guile,
           ' Sae guid and true,
' And sic a bard in a' this isle
           ' I ne'er yet knew.

' But Rab has thrown his pen awa',
' Sae I ha'e nought to do ava';
' For here the callons great and sma'
           ' Ne'er leuk at me:
' Daft fallows truly, ane and a',
           ' Compar'd wi' he.

‘ Gin 'twere no' for my Rabbie's sake,
‘ Far frae the north my course I'd take ;
‘ But frae dame Nature's child, alake !
    ‘ I downa gang,
‘ Whase canny verse o' burn and brake
     ‘ Has pleas'd me lang.

‘ For a' the live-lang simmer day
‘ Wi' him, and nane but him, I'd gae :
‘ We wander'd aft o'er birk and brae
    ‘ In ithers' spite,
‘ Where meadows green and mountains grey
     ‘ Gied him delight.

‘ Of a' my wooers Rab's the mense ;
‘ Sae tak' your pen and try for ance
‘ To praise his manly worth and sense :
    ‘ Ye may wi' truth,
‘ For flattery aft-times gi'es offence
     ‘ To age or youth.'

She turn'd her roun', but said nae mair ;
Awa' she flew I ken no' where,
Unless she sought the banks of Ayr
          To wale for ye ;
For, O ! she ca's but unco rare
          O' folk like me.

Wow man, auld Scotia mourns for ye,
And Scotia unco sad may be,
Sin Burns, wha sang wi' merry glee,
          Now quats his quill :
Rise, rise, let frien's and faes a' see
          Ye're Rabbie still.

As on some shaggy mountain's brow,
The stately oak wi' outstretch'd bough
Aye meets the passing wand'rer's view
          Afore the rest ;
E'en sae 'mang Coila's sons, I trow,
          Thou stan'st confess'd.

Prince o' the mirthfu' rhymin thrang,
Wha roam her hills and dales amang ;
Whether keen satire, tale, or sang,
   Flows frae thy pen,
Thou gi'est some lordly chiels a bang,
   Wha are but men.

Nae mair auld ALLAN gi'es delight,
Nae mair beguiles the lang mirk night,
Nor FERGUSSON, wha tried wi' might
   Dull Care to kill,
Sin' thou hast gain'd the tapmost height
   O' that fam'd hill.

How many climb, but climb in vain,
By critics aye pou'd down again ;
But where is he dare blame the strain
   O' Nature's bard,
Wha, matchless, o'er the lave doth reign,
   Without reward ?

Your name baith young and auld may bless,
Sure nane but asses can do less ;
For frae the Thames to Tweed, I guess,
   There's nane ava'
Wha read your rhymes, but maun confess
   Ye beat them a'.

This warld's a lottery, Rab, we find,
And Fortune's aft to Virtue blind,
To Merit fause, to dunces kind—
   Ye ken it's true ;
For, gin the dame true worth wou'd mind,
   She'd smile on you.

Yet tho' the hizzie's whyles severe,
E'en let her frown, we need no' fear :
Whilst I've a frien', whase smiles can cheer
   Me when I'm ill,
I'll laugh at fools wi' a' their geer,
   Wha're wretched still.

Base jade, she's gi'en me mony a hitch,
I hate her as ane sud a witch,
And care no' tho'f I be no' rich
    A single strae,
For she's a saucy, fickle ———,
    Like mony mae.

E'en let her fly this cot o' mine,
And wait upo' the lordling fine;
Tho' off rich dainties he may dine,
    And dishes rare,
The star that on his breast doth shine
    Hides mickle care.

Now tint me, Rab, I'm thinkin soon
To gi'e a ca' in DUMFRIES town:
Aiblins some bonie afternoon
    We twa may meet;
If sae, we'se spen' a white half-crown—
    Wow, 'twill be sweet!

Wi' ye I lang to ha'e a rout ;
We'se pass ae night in mirth nae doubt ;
Haith man, we'se clink the stoup about,
            And sing and play,
And keep auld Time, the blinker, out
              Till peep o' day.

Sin' life's a journey unco short,
And poor folks are but Fortune's sport,
Wi' cheerfu' sauls let's aye resort,
            As lang's we dow ;
For they wha're sad maun suffer for't,
              Right sair I trow.

The greatest bliss thro' life we know,
Is when the tears o' pity flow
Frae some kind frien' wha shares our woe
            To mak' it less ;
Syne shiel's us frae an angry foe,
             And black distrees,

Yon peasant in his strae-roof'd cot,

Whase honest heart seems free frae spot,

Blest wi' his frien', he envies not

          The rich and great ;

Nor wou'd he change his humble lot

          For pride and state.

What signifies the gaudy crew,

Wha Ruin's gilded paths pursue ;

Gi'e me the wale o' men a few,

          Wi' sense guid share,

Right honest hearts, baith leal and true,

          I ask nae mair.

May ye, dear Rab, ne'er want a friend,

Nor to chill Poverty e'er bend,

But ha'e enough to gi'e and lend

          For a' your life,

And aye be happy to your end,

          And free frae strife.

May Care, that canker, far off keep,
And Peace watch o'er ye while ye sleep ;
Syne, when in years ye 'gin to creep,
   I hope ye'll say,
Misfortune ne'er ance made ye weep,
    Nor yet leuk wae.

But had I sud ha' done lang syne,
Excuse this hodge-podge rhyme o' mine ;
And, Rab, gin ye but sen' a line,
   I vow most fervent,
I'll thank ye for't, and tak' it kine,
    Your humble servant.

CARLISLE, JUNE, 1796.

EPISTLE II.

TO A YOUTHFUL FRIEND,

WITH A COPY OF

GREGORY'S LEGACY.

HOW sweet the task to teach the tender mind
The path of Wisdom, which so few do find,
Whose ways unerring, spite of Envy's hiss,
Lead to those realms where all is endless bliss.
For this, an untaught bard, in homely strain,
To MARY sings, nor hopes he sings in vain ;
For this, the labours of the genius sends,
Who chastest pleasure with instruction blends ;
Whose moral precepts, free from pompous art,
Improve the manners as they mend the heart ;
Who joins pure diction with each classic grace,
Striving the thorny paths of Vice to trace—
A wise preceptor to the human race.

Now, when the flow'rs are welcom'd forth by spring
And in each grove the woodland warblers sing,
Let these remind thee of that Pow'r above,
Who daily shews to man his wond'rous love :
Know, 'tis his goodness that the cultur'd fields
A plenteous produce to the peasant yields.
When frowning Winter bends the naked tree,
Still praise Him who is bountiful to thee,
And look with pity on the suffering poor,
Who're doom'd full many a bitter storm t' endure :
Think, when thou see'st imploring Misery roam,
Misfortune may have robb'd him of a home ;
Nor dare to scorn Affliction's lowly cot,
Lest humbler poverty should be thy lot ;
Nor grudge the fainting wanderer relief,
But learn to feel for those o'erwhelm'd with grief,
And give with pleasure what thou canst afford,
For what thou giv'st is lent but to the Lord,
Who marks each action and its various cause,
Each pitying sigh forc'd by another's woes,

At whose all-wise command we first draw breath,
And with a Christian's hopes rejoice in death.

Whilst in thy youth, seek the true God to know,
And the pure joys which from Religion flow,
Whose sacred precepts teach weak man to shun,
The various ills by which he's oft undone.
If Virtue, that bright gem, adorn thy breast,
Ne'er envy Folly's children gaily dress'd,
Nor grieve tho' wealth and luxury be not thine,
But know thyself, nor at God's will repine :
Whate'er thy station, 'tis thy duty still
To bend submissive to his holy will.
In hours of sickness his great name adore,
Whose goodness can Health's roseate bloom restore;
And should'st thou taste life's bitter cup of care,
With fortitude thy painful sufferings bear,
Nor fail this best of maxims to regard,
That patient Virtue gains a sure reward.

Still let thy walk be heav'nly Wisdom's way,
Nor be by false-nam'd Pleasure led astray,
For Vice oft lurks in Pleasure's gayest bow'r,
And lures th' unwary at th' unguarded hour:
So the fair rose that opens with the morn,
Beneath its sweets conceals a piercing thorn.

Beware of Pride, that gay delusive guest,
The vain disturber of the artless breast;
A dang'rous pois'ner of the human mind,
Engend'ring half the evils of mankind:
'Tis Vice's ratsbane, Virtue to destroy,
Scorn'd by the righteous as a gilded toy;
A badge that tells the foolish from the wise,
Which fair Religion warns thee to despise.

Beware of artful Flattery, foe to youth,
That oft misleads you from the search of Truth;
Nor vainly boast that you are good or fair,
But let improvement be your constant care;

And if some faults in others thou should'st see,

Think others may those faults perceive in thee.

Let 'not thy tongue the innocent betray,

And deem it right thy parents to obey ;

Think how they rear'd thee in thy infant state,

And taught thy tongue Heav'n's wonders to relate :

Observe that honour which to them is due,

And with thy happiness keep theirs in view.

In all thy ways be faithful to thy trust ;

Remember God commands thee to be just.

Avoid all quarrelling and contentious strife,

For meek Religion loves the peaceful life.

Shun those who the Creator's word deride,

And let his holy scripture be thy guide ;

Then shalt thou, when old age steals on, survey

The num'rous pleasures of life's well-spent day,

And thy Redeemer's sacred promise claim,

Dying lamented with unsullied fame.

CARLISLE, APRIL, 1797.

EPISTLE III.

TO A FRIEND IN LONDON.

Cauld bla's the blast o' wild December,
Frownin Skiddaw's clad in sna'.;
Owre heartsom ingle I remember
Youthfu' days—frien's far away.

H OW late in bloom shone ilka flow'r,
How gay the woodbine form'd a bow'r ;
How sweet the breeze that wafted owre
              The sunny plain,
Enlivnin, at the mid-day hour,
              The cheerfu' swain.

But, O ! nae mair by mornin grey
O'er dewy meads he bends his way,

To hail the smilin God o' day ;
    Nor to his ear
The laverock pours his pleasing lay,
    Sae saft and clear.

Nae mair at eve, when a' is still,
He listens to the tinklin mill,
Nor marks the sun-beams gild the hill,
    Or kiss the flood ;
Nae mair the mavis, sweet but shrill,
    Rings thro' the wood.

Now angry Winter lays in waste
The meads, by dainty Simmer grac'd,
Where aft the goddess Health I chas'd,
    Far frae the crowd ;
Or strove, wi' Ednam's bard *, to taste
    Sweet Solitude.

* Thomson.

Shut up by raging storms severe
In lowly cot, the winds I hear,
And pity those wha're doom'd to bear
                    Misfortune's frown,
Wha, houseless, shed the painfu' tear,
                    To Pride unknown.

Pensive I turn to youth, life's spring,
When Fancy flutter'd on the wing,
And blythe we took in Pleasure's ring
                    An active part,
Lang ere Reflection's painfu' sting
                    Could wound the heart.

Wi' thee I spent life's golden age,
Wi' thee aft mock'd keen Winter's rage,
In harmless mirth aye proud t' engage,
                    And cheat the night ;
Or turn'd owre mony a pleasing page
                    Wi' dear delight.

Yes! Memory aye turns back to view
The scenes fond Fancy decks anew,
When we twa younkers, leal and true,
    Knew nought o' Care,
But Hope a flattering picture drew,
    In colours fair.

Then maun sic pleasures be forgot,
Ere manhood's sorrows were our lot?
Say, doth Remembrance haunt the spot
    Where youth was spent,
When Fortune's frown we heeded not,
    Led by Content?

Say, could'st thou quit the busy scene
To taste o' rural joys serene,
Sporting wi' Health the meadows green,
    Where Cauda flows,
Where aft sae merry we ha'e been,
    And free frae woes?

And wilt thou own him yet a friend,

Wha, distant, wou'd on thee depend,

And whyles thy wholsome counsel lend

His heart to cheer?

If sae, a lang Epistle send

Afore neist year.

CARLISLE, DEC. 1797.

EPISTLE IV.

TO A YOUNG LADY.

FAR, far from thee this heart holds dear,
Methinks I see the glist'ning tear
   That dimm'd thy sparkling eye :
How long must ling'ring Memory tell
Of that sad hour thou bad'st farewell,
   How long record each sigh !

Can I forget thy magic charms,
Whilst Love this tender bosom warms,
   And guides my wand'ring way ?
Ah, no ! fond Memory loves to trace
The graceful form and matchless face
   That did this heart betray.

M

When dusky Eve steals o'er the plain,
Gladd'ning the jocund village train,
 And Mirth loud-pealing strays,
Then Fancy sees thee join the throng,
And lead the sportive dance along,
 Whilst rustics on thee gaze.

Forlorn I tread each well-known round,
Where late with thee Content was found—
 Thy image meets me there :
From thee no pleasure can I prize,
From thee I spend the hours in sighs,
 And think of joys that were.

Nymph of the woodlands, Solitude,
Who fliest care-haunted Riot rude,
 And seek'st the lonely dell,
Oft list'ning, at the close of day,
To the wild-warbling linnet's lay,
 With thee, O ! let me dwell.

With thee the sorrow-clouded mind
Can taste the pleasures undefin'd,
  Which Contemplation gives :
Secluded from man's prying sight,
Oft let me feel that pure delight
  While youthful Fancy lives ;

And pensive mark the moon's pale beam,
'That, sporting o'er some dimpl'd stream,
  Beguiles Love's tedious hours,
When soft is heard the soothing tale
Of philomel, who thro' the vale
  Her song of sadness pours.

Sweet are her step-arresting notes,
That on the gentle night-breeze floats
  Along the peaceful grove ;
But sweeter to her lover's ear,
When ———'s pleasing song I hear
  Of innocence and love.

Gay Health, thou loveliest blooming maid,
If wand'ring near thy moss-crown'd shade,
   Far from the haunt of Pride,
To thy heart-gladd'ning mystic spring,
To Pleasure's mirth-inviting ring,
   Do thou her footsteps guide.

Thou soother of our keenest woes,
That dwell'st where the pure streamlet flows,
   Beneath the mountain's brow,
Queen of the rosy-tinted morn!
Shield from pale Sorrow's fest'ring thorn
   The lovely maid I woo.

When next, to shun the noontide heat,
She courts thee in thy cool retreat,
   Where dr ops the willow-tree,
Pity the bright-ey'd maiden meek,
Restore the roses to her cheek,
   And bid her haste to me.

LONDON, JUNE. 1795.

EPISTLE V.

TO A LADY.

Few frien's I court—few foes I fear,
And scant o' siller, sense, and lear :
It joys me whyles, tho' in rude lays,
Deservin, modest worth to praise.

SOME chiels for fame or riches write,
Of Sense and Reason in despite,
    And 'gainst your sex wi' rancour rail ;
Shame fa' sic loons, ill may they thrive,
Wha, bent on female ruin, strive
        To rend the heart,
        A trait'rous part,
    Wi' mony a pois'ning tale.

To ithers it great joy maun gi'e
To chase the tear frae Misery's e'e ;

While hirelings flatter warldly elves,
And reeling o'er the path o' Vice,
Gain Ruin's summit in a trice;
 Then fa'ing fast,
 They find at last
Their works e'en d—n themselves.

To thee, wha Wisdom aye pursues,
To thee, fair fav'rite o' the muse,
 A hamely, artless rhyme I send,
Prayin that ane sae guid, sae fair,
May lang remain dame Virtue's care,
 And be to a',
 Baith great and sma',
Th' instructor and the friend.

O had I but the pen o' BURNS,
For whom auld Caledonia mourns,
 And ilka bardie sings wi' wae,

Or could I but like him indite,
I then a frien' cou'd aye delight,
      And proud wou'd be,
      Wi' ane like thee,
   To tune a rural lay.

Fu' aft I read thy past'ral sang,
As o'er the moor I trudg'd alang—
      Haith, few can write sae now a-days!
Sic sentiment throughout doth shine,
Sic sweetness steals thro' ilka line,
      Had Rabbie kenn'd
      Thou sae had penn'd,
   He'd gi'en thee mickle praise.

Then harken what to me befel :
I singin hamewards lost mysel',
      As mony mae ha'e done before :
Some loons wha rule this tott'rin state
Ha'e lost themsel's I trow o' late ;

Syne angry war
Mak's poor folks jar,
And quat their native shore.

Wand'rin, wha met I but the muse ;
' Hizzie,' quo' I, ' come gi'es the news :
    ' Say, whither dost thou bend thy way ?'
Quo' she, ' I'm gaun to visit ane,
' Where Hether steals thro' yonder glen :
            ' I'm fond o' she,
            ' And done wi' ye—
' I bid ye, Sir, guid day.'

I gazin listen'd while she spoke,
Thinkin forsooth she did but joke :
    ' Guid day,' quo' I, and made a bow.
Now, ha'ing stumpie, ink, and time,
Thought I, I'se try my han' at rhyme ;
            But this dull strain
            Will shew too plain
That madam told me true.

Yet for her loss I'll no' repine,
Gif she but visit aft the **Lyne,**
  Where winsome MARY strays alang:
Then may'st thou, wi' her kindly aid,
When Nature smiles in ilka shade,
      In numbers sweet
      Saft tales repeat,
  And mony a pleasin sang.

While pining in this dimsome town,
Whare ilk ane hunts his neebor down,
  And Slander daily hauds her court,
I envy aft the country life,
Where, seated far frae busy Strife,
      Content and gay,
      Time steals away
  In mirth and harmless sport.

How sweet to taste the breeze o' morn,
How sweet to wander down the burn,

When hawthorn buds bloom fair to see ;
How sweet at eve amang the broom,
When wild flow'rs lend their rich perfume,
    The mavis sings,
    The violet springs,
    And a' to pleasure thee !

The gowans glint upo' the plain,
And lightly lilts the shepherd swain—
    Unnumber'd pleasures on thee wait !
Let great anes range o'er Fashion's round,
Where true content is seldom found :
    Dame Virtue flies
    Sic fancied joys,
    And seeks the lowly state.

In Spring thou hear'st, wi' cheerfu' voice,
Ilk minstrel o' the woods rejoice ;
    Syne Simmer smiles baith far and wide :
Soon Autumn sicklies o'er the scene ;
Bleak Winter niest, wi' breath sae keen,

Bla's o'er the hill
Baith cauld and shrill,
And blasts gay Simmer's pride.

Then may'st thou, MARY, in thy spring·
Bethink thee Time is on the wing,
   Nor let beguilin Hope persuade.
To me thou seem'st a blushing rose,
Thy sweets just 'ginnin to disclose;
      And, like a flow'r,
      Thou'lt shine thy hour,
And soon ilk bloom will fade.

Sweet lass, may Virtue dwell wi' thee,
Nor Sorrow wat thy sparklin e'e;
   But, cheer'd by meek Religion's ray,
Lang may ilk action be approv'd;
Lang may'st thou live by a' belov'd;
      Syne tak' thy pen
      And rhyme again
An answer to R. A.

EPISTLE VI.

TO A YOUNG LADY,

WHO REQUESTED THE AUTHOR TO WRITE IN RHYME.

NOW, forc'd to write a lang Epistle,
It puts me in a fearfu' fistle;
And maun be trifling, by my fay,
For haith I ken no' what to say;
But when the fair my verse doth claim,
' Should I refuse—'twou'd be a shame,
Tho' weel I ken my frien' wou'd smile,
If seated near me for a while:
I write, cross out, and interline,
Then blame this brainless head o' mine;
Walk roun' the room, at pictures keek,
And think amaist to me they speak;
That BURNS aye bids me drap the pen,
Nor woo the maid I woo in vain:

Niest o'er the ingle try a rhyme—
But, lake-a-day! its loss o' time ;
Syne screw my pipe, and saftly bla',
The lass I lo'e that's far awa'.

Time was, when a coarse, tawdry jade,
Wha little knew the rhymin trade,
Whyles ca'd, and aye a welcome fan ;
Then was poor RAB a happy man :
Her visits made me prouu I trow—
But haith nae Muse comes near me now :
Yet, spite o' th' hizzies, aye I'll write,
Sae lang's it gi'es a frien' delight,
Nor care a fig for critics sour—
On folk like me they winna low'r :
As weel might eagles quat the sky
To hunt down some wee buzzing fly.

Now thirty lifeless lines are writ,
Without the aid o' sense or wit ;

Again gaes stumpie to the ink,

Again 'bout matter I maun think :

Lines thirty mae I mean to seek,

Lest ye kick up a fearfu' reek.

When frae a frien' the letter's short,

We'd hardly gi'e a thank ye for't ;

But, O ! if lang, and free frae art,

Warm aff-hand writing frae the heart,

The pleasure that it aye affords

I fain wad tell, but want the words.

Is there a moment half sae sweet,

As when, wi' langin een, we meet

The tale o' ane far, far frae hame ?

If sae, then think me much to blame.

Like some weak wand'rer tempest tost,

Or sailor when his rudder's lost,

How to proceed troth I'm perplex'd,

For scribblers write without a text.

O cou'd I but descrive the spring,

And say how sweet the birdies sing ;

How slow the trees now blossom forth,
E'en like some bashfu' son o' worth,
Wha dreads Misfortune's nipping blast,
And, blossom-like, to earth is cast :
A' this my frien' fu' weel can tell,
Wha aft has stood the blast hersel'.
Or shou'd I praise thy virtues rare,
And ca' thee fairest o' the fair,
Syne tell o' beauty, wit, and sense ;
A' this, tho' true, might gi'e offence,
And, tint me, flattery I detest—
My number's done—forgi'e the rest.

CARLISLE, APRIL, 1798.

EPISTLE VII.

TO A YOUNG LADY,

with a copy of

RELPH'S POEMS.

DO thou accept, my youthful friend,
This gift of gratitude I send ;
A bouquet of poetic flow'rs,
Cull'd from the Muses' fav'rite bowers,
Where no unpolish'd, 'wild'ring lay
Can tempt thee from Religion's way ;
But classic wit and language clear
May feast the mind and charm the ear.

RELPH, far remov'd from busy strife,
Enjoy'd the sweets of " *Quiet Life*†,"

---

† See Relph's Poems.

And tun'd in peace his willing lyre,
Whose " wood-notes wild" all, all admire.
Tho' now no more the Muses tread
Where Fancy deck'd her Poet's head,
Yet pensive shepherds haunt the spring
Where first the youth was taught to sing;
And oft at eve the village maid
Decks with wild flow'rs the hallow'd shade,
Where, to each youthful folly blind,
He wisely strove t' improve the mind,
Nor deem'd his labours e'er misspent,
But sought in " every state content†."

With care peruse the modest bard,
And, O ! each moral well regard,
Whether the virtuous precept shine
In his or in Pythagoras' line‡ ;

---

† Make me in every state content.   RELPH.
‡ Relph's Translation of Pythagoras' Golden Verses.

For to the man our praise is due
Who Nature's rural scenery drew,
Where Virtue might her image view;
Whose songs beguile the winter night,
And artless shepherds still delight;
Whose pious lessons, and whose last address ||,
'Teach mankind how to gain " *True Happiness* *."

CARLISLE, NOV. 1797.

|| His Farewell Address to his Pupils.   See his Life.
* See his poem bearing that title.

EPISTLE VIII.

TO A FRIEND, IN THANKS FOR HIS LETTER.

DEAR Jock, I thank ye for your Letter,
And own mysel' your humble debtor :
Yet, tho' I dinna like to flatter,
        It merits praise,
For haith I ne'er receiv'd a better
        In a' my days.

Troth lad, it gied me sic delight,
I cou'd nae sleep a wink that night,
In honey words ye sae indite
        A line to me :
I'd gi'e my Sunday-coat to write
        Sic lines to ye.

Ye've seen nae doubt a wee bit boy
Pleas'd wi' a baubee or a toy;
Just sae this heart o' mine wi' joy
   Did beat fu' fain;
For lang I wonder'd ye were coy,
   I tell ye plain.

I read your kindly offers a',
And drank t' ye at the *Hole i' th' Wa'*,
Where mony a canty callan bra',
   Wha liquor lo'es,
To crack a wee will gi'e a ca',
   And hear the news..

Haith, friend, for friends, alake! are few,
Yet those I ha'e seem kind as true;
To them my best o' thanks are due
   For offers kind;
And, tent me, JOCK, a friend in you
   I'm proud to find.

How cheerly thro' this life we pass,
Troth things rub on as smooth as glass,
When, far frae a' the busy class,
   We find a friend;
But aft, o'er aft, on man, alas!
   We can't depend.

Five simmers, Jock, ha'e now flown by,
Sin' Hope bade me my fortune try;
I thank'd the dame, fu' proud was I,
   And aff I came
To this great place, where mony hie
   In quest o' fame.

They think no' vice is here a trade;
They think no' Virtue, sonsy maid,
To shew her face is aft afraid
   Upo' the street,
Where fashion, folly, and parade
   Mak' men leuk great.

O' this I'm tir'd, and think or lang
To leave it a', be't right be't rang,
For frae this bustle, noise, and thrang
                    I wish to gae ;
Aiblins, my lad, I'se northward gang,
                    I downa say ;

But hope we'se range the woods in spring,
And listen while the lintwhites sing ;
Syne pipe till glens wi' echoes ring
                    Right merrily :
Troth I'd be happier than a king
                    Were I wi' ye.

When Boreas bla's o'er hill and dale,
And nipping frosts gar folk leuk pale,
While some against their neebors rail
                    Wi' bitter spite,
We'll o'er the ingle tell a tale
                    To pass the night.

Jock, life's but like a simmer day,
Sae let's be merry while we may,
For soon a debt we a' maun pay
                    To tyrant Death,
The honest poor, the knaves so gay,
                    However laith.

Let fickle Fortune slight me still,
We maun submit do what she will :
Sin' whining does nae good but ill,
                    I'll no' despair ;
While I've my lassie, friend, and gill,
                    I dinna care.

Grown wearied o' a single life,
May ye be happy wi' your wife,
And, seated far frae noise and strife,
                    Aye live in peace ;
And as yer geer 'gins to grow rife,
                    May joys increase.

I ken ye'll think it time to end
This dull Epistle I ha'e penn'd :
Lang may ye live a poor man's friend,
             And plenty ha'e ;—
But, Jock, be sure a line aft send
             Yer friend R. A.

LONDON, 1795.

Sonnets.

SONNETS.

SONNET I.

TO J. C. CURWEN, ESQ. M. P.

He who contends for freedom
Can ne'er be justly deem'd his sovereign's foe.
THOMSON.

NOT the misnomer'd hero's praise I sing,
Who basely triumphs when he thins mankind;
Nor his who, to a people's interest blind,
The hard-earn'd mite from Industry doth wring;—
CURWEN, whose deeds a loftier verse doth claim!
CURWEN her champion Cumbria hails with pride,
And bids her son resound his deathless fame!
To him belongs the honest patriot's name,
Who strives to stem Corruption's swelling tide,
And " feels resentment for his country's shame."
Thee Independence proudly calls her own,
Who with yon recreant crew dares to contend,
Regardless or of place or placemen's frown—
Go on, great patriot, proving thou art Britain's friend!

SONNET II.

TO THE LARK.

HOW sweet in May to trace the flow'ry lawn,
　When full-blown blossoms deck the spangl'd thorn,
When, soaring from thy nest at early dawn,
　Thy sprightly matin hails the blushing morn!
To hear thee welcome forth the new-born day
　I love to range the dewy meads among.
How can the sluggard doze his time away,
　Unheedful of thy early dulcet song!
Say, whither dost thou wing thy feeble flight,
　When hoary Winter robes the fields in snow?
Poor bird!—yet are thy little cares but light
　Compar'd with his by Poverty kept low;
For, ah! no change of season cheers the sight,
　When weary life seems but a vale of woe.

SONNET III.

TO AN AGED PARENT, ON SEEING HIM SHED TEARS.

When men once reach their autumn, sickly joys
Fall off apace, as yellow leaves from trees,
At ev'ry little breath Misfortune blows.   YOUNG.

FOND Parent, whom on earth I love most dear,

Why steals that sigh of sadness from thy breast?

I too do grieve to see thee sore oppress'd,

Whilst down thy care-worn cheek steals many a tear!

Thou weep'st, my father!—the sad cause I guess:

Long hast thou journey'd o'er life's mazy wild,

A sorrowing traveller, by false Hope beguil'd,

And few there be who pity thy distrees;

Nor Plenty on thy cot hath ever smil'd.

Robb'd of the blissful partner of each hour,

All thy self-promis'd joys, alas! are fled;

On thee life's wintry storms begin to low'r,

And thou dost bend.   So fades the summer flow'r

At winter's keen approach, and droops its feeble head.

SONNET IV.

WRITTEN IN WINTER.

CHILL blows the raging blast across the plain,
  And sickly Phœbus scarce a ray sends forth ;
  Keen Winter now steals from the angry north,
And from the meadow drives the shepherd swain,
Who, tempest-beaten, in his snow-clad cot,
  Listens with horror to the howling wind ;
Yet calm Contentment cheers his humble lot—
  Contentment known but to the virtuous mind.
Tho' now no flow'rets deck yon brambl'd glade,
  Where sweet the blackbird sung his evening lay ;
Tho' leafless now the oak that form'd a shade
  To rustic lovers at the close of day ;
Yet Winter's angry howl and dark'ning gloom
Sad Sorrow soothes more than gay Summer's bloom.

SONNET V.

TO A ROSE IN ELIZA'S BOSOM.

THOU sweetest flow'r that decks the enamell'd bed,
    Say, little rival, by my love confess'd,
Why dost thou hide thy sweets and droop thy head,
    Why fade so near ELIZA's snowy breast?
When May return'd with all her sportive train,
    I saw thee budding in thy fragrant seat—
O that 'twere mine the lily hand to gain
    That gently pluck'd thee from thy lone retreat!
Hail, blushing Rose! an emblem of my fair,
    In thee ELIZA's sweetness let me trace;
Thy bloom the beauty that adorns her face,
Thy fragrant smell her breath that scents the air:
Sweet flow'r! thy beauties bloom but for a day,
Just like her charms, that ere life's eve must fade away!

SONNET VI.

TO A YOUNG LADY, WITH SOME SONGS IN MANUSCRIPT.

FOR thee I cull no fair poetic flow'rs,
   By Genius borrow'd from th' inspiring Muse;
Tho' oft her votary at the evening hours,
As pensive wand'ring near her peaceful bow'rs,
   Yet she, coy nymph, her aid did still refuse.
Her smile no longer courting, thus I said—
   ' The world will tell in vain I waste my time
   ' Weaving in lowly cot my humble rhyme:
' Yes!—I will straight pursue some kinder maid,
   ' Nor envy him who soars in bold sublime.'
Then Fancy thy fair form did quick present:
   To thee I send my artless songs of love;
Nor will I think one hour hath been misspent,
   Should thou, sweet maid, one artless song approve.

SONNET VII.

EVENING.

MILD Evening's floating breeze perfumes the air,
Whilst blushing Phœbus hastens down the west;
The twitt'ring swallow seeks her peaceful nest,
And home the rustic turns his bleating care.
Now from the drooping violet in the glade
The zephyrs sweet their balmy course pursue;
To distant sloping hills embrown'd in shade
The parting sun now bids a short adieu;
The shepherd's pipe proclaims the sportive dance,
And calls the younker from his daily toil;
Upon the green the village swains advance,
In harmless mirth the moments to beguile.
Hail, rural sweets, that charm the pensive Muse,
As she her contemplative flow'ry path pursues!

SONNET VIII.

TO JOHN HORNE TOOKE, ESQ.

⸻———" May he live
" Longer than I have time to tell his years."

CHAMPION of freedom, friend to all mankind,
   Let Britons hail the day which gave thee birth ;
Thou who would'st guide with truth the erring mind,
   And crown with peace all nations of the earth.
Ne'er didst thou, TOOKE, swerve from the public weal;
   Ne'er didst thou climb Ambition's tow'ring height ;
Corruption trembles at thy manly zeal,
   As sinks Oppression at the hero's might.
When Gallia's sons shook off despotic pow'r,
   And from their clime fell Superstition hurl'd,
Thou, Britain's Patriot ! didst proclaim the hour
   When heav'n-born Freedom smil'd upon the world.
Long shall thy suff'rings tell thy country's shame,
And long fair Virtue's sons shall venerate thy name.

SONNET IX.

TO THE RIVER EDEN.

~~~~~~

And dwell with fond delay on blessings past. SHAW.

━━━━━

THOU murm'ring emblem of a troubled mind,

  That wak'st fond Memory's tear, for ever true !

Time was, when, on thy moss-grown bank reclin'd,

I view'd thy surface ruffled by the wind,

  As eager, light-wing'd Fancy forward flew ;

Then did I dream of joys I ne'er could find—

  'Twas life's gay spring, and sorrows were but few.

Sweet stream ! whose mournful melody is dear,

  Far from fell Slander and her wolfish brood !

A wand'rer oft, thy flow'r-clad margin near,

  I'll pensive think of man's ingratitude ;

And youth's gay age, when Mirth oft led me here,

Ere Mis'ry bade me drop the painful tear,

  Or Hope, with flatt'ring tale, this bosom did delude.

SONNET X.

TO A REDBREAST, WHICH VISITED THE AUTHOR DAILY FOR SOME MONTHS.

WRITTEN NOV. 1796.

DOMESTIC songster of the waning year,
  I bid thee welcome, and thy wild notes greet;
Altho' they tell th' approach of winter drear,
  No artful concerts to mine ear so sweet!
Emblem of Poverty! how hard thy fate
  When the wild tempests scowl along the sky!
E'en now methinks thou wail'st thy absent mate,
  Singing thy love-lorn song :—just so do I.
Peace to the bard*, who, taught by Nature's law,
  From tyrant man at once could set thee free:
Oft have I read his plaintive tale of woe,
  Oft shed a tear for Innocence and thee.
Come then, sweet bird! nor wander to and fro,
  Welcome to share this humble roof with me.

* Author of the Norfolk Tragedy.

SONNET XI.

TO THE SAME.

WRITTEN MARCH, 1797.

Now angry Winter's breath is felt no more,
 And hush'd the blast that rag'd the woods along;
Thou welcome partner of my scanty store,
 Dost give thy little all—a cheerful song,
Sweet is that song of gratitude to me,
 Tho' oft methinks each note doth bid adieu.
Poor bird! would man to man but prove so true
Thro' life's rough voyage as I have been to thee,
 How cheerly mortals might their path pursue,
Who sink beneath the load of poverty!
Tho' thy wild minstrelsy to me is dear,
 Yet go thy ways, fond wand'rer, seek the grove;
 Spring calls thee forth—go taste the joys of love;
And when wild Autumn Summer's sweets shall sear,
 Revisit then my cot —again I'll prove
Thy friend, and shield thee from the storm severe.

＼ SONNET XII.

TO A YOUNG LADY LABOURING UNDER A
SEVERE ILLNESS.

EMBLEM of Innocence, the Snowdrop meek,
    Around in early spring its fragrance pours ;
The firstling fair bends from the wild winds bleak,
    Recov'ring with the genial noon-tide hours.
So, child of Virtue! didst thou pour thy song,
    By Nature taught, in Solitude's lone grove,
    Breathing sweet lays of innocence and love,
Thy " wild notes" charming oft the list'ning throng,
Till pale Disease, to whom e'en kings must bend,
    Stole from thy cheek Health's fairest blushing rose:
    Yet grieve not, since that Pow'r who marks thy woes
His sorrow-soothing balm to thee may lend,
Bidding those virtues yet a while to bloom,
That, by Religion led, can triumph o'er the tomb.

SONNET XIII.

TO A POOR BOY.

Thrice happy they who sleep in humble life,
Beneath the storm Ambition blows.   YOUNG.

MEEK child of Want! I pity thy distress,

For I have learn'd to feel another's woe;

Yes,—my heart pants to make thy sorrows less,

And dry the tear which Mis'ry bids to flow.

Ye, whom nor cold nor pining hunger press,

Nor frowning Poverty's sad anguish know,

What boots it that ye shine like insects gay,

The vain, unthinking parasites of pow'r!

How oft doth syren Vice lead you astray,

How oft embitter Pleasure's gayest hour!

Tho' never thou enjoy'st the plenteous meal,

Tho' tatter'd thy coarse weeds, yet, poor forlorn!

Sooner thy keenest sorrows would I feel,

Than be the son of Wealth that mocks thy woes

with scorn!

SONNET XIV.

TO ELIZA.

~~~

And banished I am if but from thee. SHAKESPEARE.

O Lovely Maid, whose bosom knows no guile!
Enchanting fair, that robs me of my rest!
Fond Fancy traces oft thy heav'nly smile,
    Which rais'd a passion in this peaceful breast.
Tho' distant from the place I hold so dear,
    I ne'er forget those joys I knew of late;
But, like the dove who mourns his absent mate,
Pining in grief, love prompts the painful tear.
Lonely I range the briary woods along,
    Where Nature's wildness charm'd my infant view;
Pensive I hear at noon the woodlark's song—
    Still busy Memory paints our last adieu;
For what avails to me the beauties of the grove,
Since I am doom'd to mourn far from the maid I love!

SONNET XV.

TO A PRETENDED FRIEND.

Know'st thou, Lorenza, what a friend contains? YOUNG.

SINCE all are wand'rers o'er life's dreary waste,
If, faint and weary, by the path-way side,
I saw a fellow-traveller in distress,
Tho' weak, I would stretch forth my feeble arm
To help him on—nor deem the time misspent.
So thou hast said full oft ; but, when pale Want,
Unwelcome visitor ! with pallid eye,
Came stalking in upon me, thou wert fled.
Thus the poor seaman, on the stormy deep,
Sees dangers press; and, by the fancied land
Lur'd from his wonted course, he sighs and sinks.
Yet may chill Poverty ne'er be thy lot,
Nor thou e'er taste Misfortune's bitter draught,
But drink the cup thou would'st not hold to others.

R

SONNET XVI.

NIGHT.

NOW solemn Night her sable curtain draws,
  Pale Cynthia steals her silv'ry course along;
No noise disturbs the villager's repose,
  Save philomel, who mourns in plaintive song.
The scatter'd prospects on the distant plain,
  The lofty tow'rs that draw the wand'rer nigh,
  Are hid in darkness from the busy eye,
Since awful Night's assum'd her silent reign.
The whisp'ring breeze that gently sweeps the dale,
  The roaring surge that courts the rising wind,
  Now soothe a while the contemplative mind,
In wand'ring thro' life's solitary vale;
Whilst the twinkling stars, and cheering orb of night,
Point out to feeble man his great Creator's might.

SONNET XVII.

TO THE RIVER CALDEW.

THO' down thy silv'ry current, winding stream,
  Proud Commerce ne'er doth bend the swelling sail ;
Tho' seldom thou hast been the poet's theme ;
  Yet canst thou boast of many a bowery vale,
The wood umbrageous and the flow'r-wov'n glade,
  Where Health's pure breeze steals on each fragrant
And near thy banks the artless village maid   [gale ;
  Blooms fair as those by Yarrow, Tay, or Tweed ;
Nor sings the linnet sweeter in the shade
  Where Twick'nham's minstrel tun'd his rapt'rous
O were the art of poesy but mine,   [reed.
  Known to the bard* who trod thy willowy shore,
Then should'st thou flow in many a polish'd line ;—
  But dull the lay whose author knows no classic lore!

* Mr. Thomas Sanderson.

R 2

SONNET XVIII.

TO MR. ROBERT CARLILE.

Full many a flow'r is born to blush unseen,
And waste its sweetness on the desert air. GRAY.

ACCEPT, O youthful Bard! the humble lays
Of one who'd fain thy modest worth proclaim:
Could I in tuneful numbers sing thy praise,
   My soaring muse should tell the world thy fame.
Hail, Nature's child! (whom Learning's sons admire)
   She taught thee how to paint each scene with art† ;
She taught thee how to tune th' harmonious lyre,
   And strike the finest feelings of the heart.
Like thee, I've seen the tender budding rose
   Hiding its sweetness from refreshing show'rs,
Blushing its infant beauties to expose,
   Till ripen'd age call'd forth its op'ning pow'rs:
Then may thy genius like a rose burst forth,
And Britain boast thy name among her sons of worth.

† Alluding to the rural drawings of this young artist.

SONNET XIX.

TO ELIZA.

THE grief-worn wand'rer, forc'd afar to roam,

Beholds each object with an aching eye ;

Cheerless and sad he heaves the rending sigh,

If Memory point but to his native home,

And pines for what he ne'er can hope to gain.

So have I lonely wander'd, sweetest maid !

And seen gay Spring call forth each fav'rite flow'r,

Seen rip'ning Summer form the woodbine bow'r,

As, press'd with care, I sought the peaceful shade,

What time grey Eve stole o'er the dewy plain.

Then oft the blackbird, from the brambl'd glade,

His love-lorn song, like me, did plaintive pour :

But cheerful Spring, nor Summer's festive hour,

Could charm, if Fancy thy fair form pourtray'd.

SONNET XX.

WRITTEN IN SPRING.

AGAIN gay Spring the rustic calls to love,
And spreads her flow'ry mantle o'er the grove;
  The soaring lark again salutes the morn,
And sings to Phœbus oft a cheerful strain;
  At eve the ploughman views his rising corn,
And hears soft music echo o'er the plain:
But, ah! gay Spring removes not keen Despair,
Nor soothes the wretched bosom fraught with care!
Whether I seek the thick embow'ring shade,
  Or thro' the dasied meadow bend my way,
I court in vain the joys Hope once pourtray'd—
  Her fairest blossoms bloom but to decay:
Tir'd Fancy now a gloomy picture draws,
And Sadness round my head her faded garland throws.

SONNET XXI.

TO AN UNFORTUNATE FEMALE.

And one false step entirely damns her name. ROWE.

F RIENDLESS, unpitied wand'rer of the night,
The scorn of Pride, who seldom learns to feel,
O that thy painful suff'rings I could heal,
And shield thee from a world too apt to slight!
Dead are the blushes that did once adorn
The cheek of Virtue, some fond parent's pride,
Who dreamt not syren Pleasure, in life's morn,
From Virtue's path would draw thy steps aside.
And shall Misfortune then make vice a law?
Must bleeding Innocence steal from thy breast?
Shall thy keen sorrows banish Peace and Rest,
And calm Reflection come too late?—Ah, no!
Thou child of Misery, of each joy bereft,
Religion's saving comfort yet for thee is left!

SONNET XXII.

LET others praise the splendour of the town,
  Where Wealth unfeeling, Misery doth deride;
Where patient Merit seldom gains renown,
  But sinks beneath the bitter taunt of Pride,
And Virtue pines in want; while Vice on down
  Sees pamper'd Folly fatt'ning by her side.
Tho' Grandeur scorns me, and my cot be rude;
  Tho' doom'd to tread thro' life a thorny way;
Tho' the fair flow'rs, by youthful Fancy strew'd,
  Ere manhood's prime, had hasten'd to decay,
And on my steps doth Sorrow aye intrude,
  Dark'ning the light of Hope's heart-cheering ray;
Yet fain with thee I'd dwell, sweet SOLITUDE,
  And, far from Riot, wait life's closing day.

Songs.

SONGS.

SONG I.

A LASSIE AND A GILL.

Tune—" O'er Bogie."

LET Fortune smile on Impudence,
  And to the dunce prove kind ;
Gi'e me the chiel wi' common sense
  And independent mind,
    Wha can agree
    ·Wi' Poverty,
  _ And be contented still,
Wha ilka night delights to see
  His Lassie and his Gill.

By Hope, that will-o'-th'-wisp, we're led—
  To youth her aid she lends ;

But when ilk golden prospect's fled,
   And man to poortith bends,
      The warl will frown,
      And haud him down,
   In spite o' Reason's skill:
E'en then life's sweetness are his own,
   A Lassie and a Gill.

Let Grandeur tak' the gilded wa's,
   And frae poor Merit fly,
There's still ae charm that a' his ha's
   And filthy gowd can't buy:
      In palace pent,
      Knows he content,
   Like Hab wha tends the mill,
Wha smiles at ills he can't prevent—
   His Lassie and his Gill.

Sin' warly riches canna gain
   A day, nor yet an hour,

A fig for Wealth and a' her train,

Let's be content tho' poor,

And laugh at Care,

And black Despair,

And mak' Time cheerie still;

When thus, we need but twa things mair,

A Lassie and a Gill.

SONG II.

THE CAPTIVE.

Y ES, he is blest, who for the fair
    Heaves not the fond impassion'd sigh;
Who heeds not beauty, shape, or air,
    Nor knows the language of the eye.

But pity to the wretch is due,
    Who, love-beguil'd, still loves in vain;
Who seems a phantom to pursue,
    Yet, hope-inspir'd, pursues with pain:

Whose looks betray the bursting heart,
    That vainly pants for liberty:
Death only takes the mourner's part,
    Who sets the wearied Captive free.

SONG III.

MARIAN.

WHY dowie and sad sits poor Marian,
  And why steal the tears frae her e'e?
The flow'rs that in spring time were blooming,
  Bloom'd nae half sae bonie to see.

Wha ance was sae blythe as Marian,
  Wha danc'd half sae light on the green;
But now a' the lave weep, sin' Marian
  Nae mair with the younkers is seen.

The flocks on the hills are a' sporting,
  The gowdspink sings sweet on the spray;
While Marian sits wailing where Sandy
  Aft pip'd at the close of the day.

Nae mair in the hairst, at the sheering,

The jokes and the blythe tales are told ;

Nae music is heard in the loanings,

When wearing the sheep to the fold.

O ! dool tak' the loons, whase ambition

Sends lads frae the lasses awa',

And mak's Marian weep by the burnie

For Sandy, the flower o' them a' !

SONG IV.

GENEROUS WINE.

What wonders cannot Wine effect?—'Tis free
Of secrets, and turns hope to certainty. CREECH.

THOU sportive charmer, ever gay,
   Whose blushing sweets and radiant smile
Can chase the canker Care away,
   And Sorrow of her thorn beguile!
No more I heed fair JULIA's eye,
   No more I seek to press her lip,
No more her frown shall prompt a sigh,
   Whilst I thy cheering sweets can sip:
Her fading charms I pleas'd resign,
Since thou'rt my mistress, generous Wine!

Let Fortune's vot'ries round her press,
   And Folly's sons her favours own;

T

How few the goddess deigns to bless,

How many sink beneath her frown!

Vain mortals! wealth for you can't buy

Health's roseate hue, or lasting peace,

Nor cheat the bosom of a sigh—

For riches but our cares increase:

Nor Love nor Wealth shall make me pine,

Whilst thou'rt my mistress, generous Wine!

SONG V,

BEN BOWSER'S MAXIM.

BEN Bowser was valiant, a true British tar,
Had brav'd ev'ry danger in tempest or war;
Was content as an emp'ror, tho' ever so poor,
And would sigh at the hardships too many endure:
To his friend ever gen'rous, to Bess ever true,
Ben still did to others as he'd be done to.

'What a pity,' cried Ben, ' that, in sailing thro' life,
' There are lubbers so fond of base jarring and strife;
' How snug might us steer thro' life's billowy sea,
' If all hands to each other as brethren would be:
' What a pity,' he'd cry, ' that the number's so few,
' Who do unto others as they'd be done to.'

Tho' light was his heart, he of grief had his share,
Yet his maxim was just, ' Man ought not to despair;'

Ant your lubberly lordling who struts on dry land,

Like poor Ben, forc'd to yield at his Maker's command:

Then what argufies greatness, tho' rich as a Jew,

If he ne'er does to others as he'd be done to.

When wreck'd out at Indies, he'd shiners galore,

And many a poor comrade partook of his store:

All rejoic'd he'd escap'd from a watery grave,

Who gloried in conquest, but conquer'd to save:

When a Don was blown up, like a lion he flew,

And did unto others as he'd be done to.

Return'd to Old England, half naked and poor,

He sought out his Bess, who now shew'd him the door.

By old friends quite forsaken, how painful his lot—

Those who once shar'd his gold, now, when poor,
      know him not:

Joy-deserted, a beggar the maim'd wand'rer view,

And still do to others as you'd be done to.

SONG VI.

LUCY GRAY OF ALLENDALE.

SET TO MUSIC BY MR. HOOK,

And sung by Master PHELPS, at VAUXHALL, 1794.

O HAVE you seen the blushing rose,
The blooming pink, or lily pale ;
Fairer than any flow'r that blows
Was Lucy Gray of Allendale.

Pensive and sad by brae and burn,
Where oft the nymph they us'd to hail,
The shepherds now are heard to mourn
For Lucy Gray of Allendale.

With her to join the rural dance,
Far have I stray'd o'er hill and vale ;
Then pleas'd each rustic stole a glance
At Lucy Gray of Allendale.

'Twas underneath the hawthorn shade
  I told her first the tender tale ;
But now low lays the lovely maid,
  Sweet Lucy Gray of Allendale.

Bleak blows the wind, keen beats the rain,
  Upon my cottage in the vale :
Long may I mourn a lonely swain,
  For Lucy Gray of Allendale.

SONG VII.

DONALD OF DUNDEE.

~<~<~•~>~>~

SET TO MUSIC BY MR. HOOK,

And sung by Miss MILNE, at VAUXHALL, 1795.

Y OUNG Donald is the blythest lad
　　That e'er made love to me ;
　Whene'er he's by my heart is glad,
　　He's aye so kind and free ;
　Then on his pipe he plays so sweet,
　And in his plaid he looks sae neat,
　It cheers my heart at eve to meet
　　Young Donald of Dundee.

　Whene'er I gang to yonder grove,
　　Young Davie follows me,
　And fain he wants to be my love—
　　But, ah! that canna be :

Tho' mither frets baith soon and late,

For me to wed this youth I hate,

There's nane need hope to win young Kate,

But Donald of Dundee.

When last we rang'd the banks of Tay,

The ring he shew'd to me,

And bade me name the bridal day,

Then happy wou'd he be :

I ken the youth will aye prove kind,

Nae mair my mither will I mind,

Mess John to me shall quickly bind

Young Donald of Dundee.

SONG VIII.

POOR ANNA.

POOR Anna was the shepherds' pride,
Each village maid she did excel;
Young Edwy sought her for his bride,
And lov'd her more than tongue can tell.
Young Edwy died—fair Anna strove
Her grief to hide, but no more smil'd;
Her reason fled with her true love,
And now she wanders Sorrow's child,
Twining many a gaudy flower,
Singing thus near Edwy's bower:
‘ Be still, be still, thou bursting heart!
‘ Ah, busy tear! why dost thou start?
‘ The fondest lovers soon must part.’

No more she joins upon the plain
The sportive dance at close of day;

U

Her aged parents try in vain
  Her thoughts from Edwy to betray.
At night she sits where cold he lies,
  Still promising to meet him soon,
Or thro' the vale distracted flies,
  Her sorrows telling to the moon;
Or, at the silent midnight hour,
Singing thus near Edwy's bower:
  ' Be still, be still, thou bursting heart!
  ' Ah, busy tear! why dost thou start?
  ' The fondest lovers soon must part.'

Her pallid cheek, her flowing hair,
  With chaplets of wild flow'rets drest;
Her tatter'd robe, with bosom bare,
  Bespeak the woes that pierce her breast.
Oft pensive shepherds sigh to hear
  Her fault'ring tongue sad tales relate;
While sorrowing maidens drop a tear,
  And pity hapless Anna's fate.

Twining many a faded flower,
Singing thus near Edwy's bower:
' Be still, be still, thou bursting heart!
' Ah, busy tear! why dost thou start?
' The fondest lovers soon must part.'

SONG IX.
HARK AWAY!

THIS world's a wide plain, where, like hounds in full
  Mankind are all eager the chase to pursue; [cry,
O'er the strong bounds of reason regardless they fly,
  To hunt down each other, when profit's in view;
Led on by ambition, pride, riches, or fame,
Each mortal toils hard in pursuit of his game.
    Observe life's vain fantastic crew;
    See how each hunts with game in view;
    The young, the old, the grave, the gay,
    All join the cry of hark away!

The soldier hunts honour, and flies to the war;
  The patriot's in quest of a pension or place;
At the sound of a title, a ribband, or star,
  The courtier he eagerly joins in the chase:
The doctor hunts patients, the lawyer a fee,
And a mitre's fine game grave divines all agree.
  Observe life's vain fantastic crew, &c.

In pursuit of the fashion yon pert powder'd beau
  O'er Pleasure's gay course gallops heedless along
The coquette so artful each charm tries to shew,
  And in quest of a lover still joins in the throng:
Whilst Folly starts game to amuse the gay town,
See Vice in full cry hunting poor Virtue down.
  Observe life's vain fantastic crew;
  See how each hunts with game in view:
  The young, the old, the grave, the gay,
  All join the cry of hark away!

SONG X.
DEARLY DO I LOVE THEE.

Come and live wi' me, lassie,
Bra lassie, bonie lassie,
Come and live me, lassie,
For dearly do I love thee.

WHEN simmer paints the meadows gay,
And sangsters gladden bank and brae,
Amang the broom we'll sport and play,
    For dearly do I love thee.
        Come and live wi' me, lassie, &c.

When wintry winds bla' loud and keen,
And frownin sna's on hills are seen,
I'll screw my pipe to please my Jean,
    For dearly do I love thee.
        Come and live wi' me, lassie, &c.

Tho' fickle Fortune keeps me poor,
Ambition ne'er shall cross my door;
And wert thou mine I'd ask no more,
    For dearly do I love thee.
        Come and live wi' me, lassie, &c.

But had I gowd or had I land,
Or had I kingdoms at command,
I'd gi'e them a' to gain thy hand,
    For dearly do I love thee.
        Come and live wi' me, lassie,
            Bra lassie, bonie lassie,
        Come and live wi' me, lassie,
            For dearly do I love thee.

SONG XI.
THEODORE AND ANNETTE.

ON a green shady bank as young Theodore lay,
  Lull'd to sleep by the murmuring brook,
Annette, as she carelessly wander'd that way,
  Stole his garland, his pipe, and his crook ;
Then instantly hied to a neighbouring shade,
  While unheeded her flock stray'd around ;
And so sweet was the music the shepherdess play'd,
  That all nature seem'd pleas'd with the sound.

Awak'd from his slumber, young Theodore gaz'd,
  Whilst Echo enliven'd the plain,
Then sought for his pipe ; but was strangely amaz'd,
  And thus sung his sorrowful strain :
' My wreath was an emblem of Annette the fair,
  ' The flow'rets so gay were her choice ;
' My pipe often sooth'd me when sunk in despair,
  ' As I listen'd at eve to her voice.

' How oft have I charm'd the gay nymphs in the grove,
　' Where now I may heave the sad sigh.'
Thus mourn'd the young shepherd, while Annette
　　his love
　In a thicket stood listening by :
She eagerly flew to her lover's relief ;
　He tenderly hung on her breast ;
The smiles of the maid soon dispell'd all his grief—
　Fond lovers can fancy the rest.

SONG XII.

I'SIGH FOR THE GIRL I ADORE.

SET TO MUSIC BY MR. HOOK,

And sung by Master PHELPS, at VAUXHALL, 1794.

WHEN fairies trip round the gay green,
 And all nature seems sunk into rest,
Thro' valleys I wander unseen,
 My heart with sad sorrow opprest;
And oft by the murmuring streams
 Fair Eleanor's loss I deplore,
As alone, by the moon's silver beams,
 I sigh for the girl I adore.

When my flocks wander o'er the wide plain,
 To some thicket of woodbine I rove,
There pensively tune a soft strain,
 Or sing forth the praise of my love.

x

Where does my fair Eleanor stray?
Must I ne'er see the nymph any more?
Thus distracted I mourn the long day,
And sigh for the girl I adore.

When first I beheld the sweet maid,
By moon-light alone in the vale,
Far, far from the village we stray'd,
Where I tenderly told a soft tale.
How long must I wander forlorn?
Ah! when will my sorrows be o'er?
Such grief it can never be borne—
I sigh for the girl I adore.

SONG XIII.

LUCKLESS JEAN.

WHEN War's shrill trumpet ca'd to arms,
    And Britain bade fair FREEDOM yield,
Young Collin, won by loons' alarms,
    Fled far to seek the tented field.
My heart was laith to bid adieu,
    And aft the tears stole frae my een;
Three times he cried, ' Sweet lass, be true!'
    Syne tore himself frae luckless Jean.

Blythe Spring awakes the tunefu' groves,
    And gowans glint o'er meadows gay;
While Jean unpitied lonely roves,
    And thinks o' him that's far away.
Auld Nature's smiles cou'd pleasure gi'e,
    When Collin woo'd me on the green;
Ilk season brought new joys to me;
    But Pleasure's fled frae luckless Jean.

Nae mair the blythsome lilt I hear

  O' younkers singing at the plough;

A' round me seems a desert drear,

  Where waving Plenty met my view.

Whene'er I steal alang the burn,

  Where aft sae merry we ha'e been,

Ilk mavis seems wi' me to mourn,

  Ilk lintwhite pities luckless Jean.

How lang will poor deluded man

  Against his brither dra' his sword,

To shield a base oppressive clan,

  The hireling, knave, and pamper'd lord!

Come, meek-ey'd PEACE, thy olive wave,

  Lang time a wand'rer hast thou been;

Thy smiles frae death may thousands save,

  And bring her love to luckless Jean.

SONG XIV.

Y E who would life's pleasures prove,
Taste the sweets of wine and love :
Wine, that lulls each care to rest ;
Love, that melts the tyrant's breast.

Envy not pert Fashion's fool,
Nor the few who're born to rule ;
Grandeur, Pow'r, and Wealth despise—
Gay Content far from them flies.

Heed not how the moments pass,
Fill to love the sparkling glass ;
Toast the young, the fair, the gay :
Life is short—live while you may.

SONG XV..

POLLY.

In Yarmouth first fair Poll I saw,
    Well rigg'd, tight-built, for service clever;
I hail'd and took her straight in tow,
    And vow'd to sail with her for ever :
Splic'd to a girl so fair and kind,
    The sailor knows no jealous folly;
But soon, alas! the fickle wind
    Forc'd me on board from lovely Polly.

Scarce had we put three days to sea,
    When a hard gale our vessel shatter'd;
No hopes of safety then had we,
    For all around us rocks lay scatter'd.
The lightning's flash, the thunder's roll,
    I heeded not, still brisk and jolly ;
Soon in a calm we slung the bowl ;
    Each gave his girl—I toasted Polly.

Sav'd from the storm, a ship we 'spy'd ;

    The word was giv'n, loud cannons rattle :

' Adieu, my Poll,' I sighing cried,

    ' For soon thy Ben may fall in battle.'

Tho' both my limbs were shiver'd sore,

    I thought repining nought but folly,

And boldly brav'd the battle's roar,

    Cheer'd with the hope of meeting Polly.

They struck, and soon to land we bore,

    When sailors feel a glowing pleasure ;

I flew to meet my girl on shore,

    And share with her my hard-earn'd treasure :

But in a calm the wind may veer,

    So mirth may turn to melancholy ;

A tar soon whisper'd, with a tear,

    That Death had robb'd me of my Polly.

Full oft I've fought my country's cause,

    And weather'd many a stormy ocean ;

Thro' life have borne my share of woes—
    For happiness is all a notion;
Yet, like a sailor bold and brave,
    I'll never pine in melancholy,
But do my duty, till the grave
    Makes Ben forget the charms of Polly.

SONG XVI.

COME, SWEET GIRL, AND LIVE WITH ME.

GAY Spring with flow'rs bedecks the plains,
    Soft music echoes thro' the grove;
How cheerful seem the nymphs and swains,
    And all around is mirth and love:
Earth spreads a fragrant couch for thee—
    O come, sweet girl, and live with me.

Mild Summer, smiling o'er the fields,
  Invites me to the woodbine bow'r;
Pensive I view what Summer yields,
  Pensive I cull each fav'rite flow'r;
The chaplet twin'd, I think of thee,
Then come, sweet girl, and live with me.

Rich Autumn waves her golden store,
  And saffron'd leaves fall by each blast.
Thus life's gay summer soon is o'er,
  And Memory weeps at what is past:
My wearied thoughts still turn to thee—
O come, sweet girl, and live with me.

In Winter, when the piercing wind,
  Disrobes gay Nature of her charms,
Thy fancied presence cheers my mind,
  And soothing Hope my bosom warms:
I tune my pipe to love and thee,
Then come, sweet girl, and live with me.

Y

SONG XVII.

THE LASSES O' THE LYNE.

OF Yarrow, Tweed, and winding Tay,
  Fu' lightly Allan sang, O;
To Nanny Burns aft tun'd his lay,
  Till glens wi' echoes rang, O:
In weel-tim'd verse cou'd I rehearse
  The charms o' maidens fine, O,
My sang shou'd be in praise o' three,
  The lasses o' the Lyne, O.

Ye dainty dames wi' borrow'd face,
  Whase praise but few can tell, O;
Wha proudly sneer, and scorn the place
  Where Virtue likes to dwell, O;
For you sae gay, at ball or play,
  Tho' tinsell'd beaus may pine, O,
Your town-bred air can no compare
  Wi' the lasses o' the Lyne, O.

To warldly elves gi'e gowd and land,
  To courtly knaves gi'e pride, O ;
A' India's wealth cou'd I command,
  I'd dwell by yon burn side, O.
Sin' Poverty aye hauds by me,
  Sic joys can ne'er be mine, O ;
In artless lays content I'll praise
  The lasses o' the Lyne, O.

SONG XVIII.

FAIR SALLY.

WHEN Honour bade her sons bear arms,
  And boldly meet their country's foe,
I saw in vain fair Sally's charms,
  Adown whose cheeks the tears did flow ;
And wearied with the rural life,
  The russet hill and flowery dale,
Won by the drum and sprightly fife,
  Elate I left my native vale.

The toils of war long time I brav'd,
  Of danger still I bore a share,
And many a foe this arm hath sav'd,
  For man may conquer, yet should spare.
Such scenes of carnage pall'd my mind;
  Soon Britain's coast I long'd to hail,
And thought of joys I left behind,
  When Fancy sought my native vale.

Oft have I pray'd that war would cease,
  When bleeding brethren clad the plain,
And soon the tidings of sweet Peace
  Brought toil-worn warriors home again,
Discharg'd, dread war a while forgot,
  Fair Sally soon I hop'd to hail,
And onward trudg'd towards her cot,
  O'erjoy'd to view my native vale.

I pass'd the oak, beneath whose shade,
  I of fair Sally took my leave;

I pass'd the grove where, with the maid,

 The happy hours were spent at eve ;

I pass'd the village church—but wept,

 And trembling read the plain-told tale,

That underneath fair Sally slept,

 For one who left his native vale.

SONG XIX.

ELIZA.

ERE fair Eliza's face I knew,

 Contentment crown'd my cot ;

My cares seem'd light, my wants were few,

 Vain pomp I envied not :

The rosy hours flew swift away,

 I pip'd with merry glee ;

No lark that hail'd the rising day

 Was half so gay or free.

Remembrance paints the pleasing scene,
  When first she won my heart;
Her beauteous face, her comely mein,
  Shone unadorn'd by art:
Now lonely wand'ring thro' the grove,
  This bosom fill'd with care,
I tune my pipe to hapless love,
  And mourn my absent fair.

The wretch enslav'd on Afric's coast,
  More freedom knows than I;
Content is fled, blest Peace is lost,
  In vain I heave the sigh:
Come then, sweet Hope, and soothe my grief,
  Thy smiles oft cheer my breast;
'Tis thou alone canst give relief,
  And make a lover blest.

SONG XX.

BONNY JEM THAT'S O'ER THE SEA.

SET TO MUSIC BY MR. HOOK,

And sung by Mrs. FRANKLIN, at VAUXHALL, 1796.

Y OUNG Jemmy was a Highland lad,
    That oft-times cross'd the burn to me;
He wore the bonnet, trows, and plaid,
    Wi' garters green below his knee :
Of a' the shepherds west the Tweed,
By ilka ane it is agreed,   .
There's nane cou'd tune the oaten reed,
    Like bonny Jem that's o'er the sea.

May ill befa' the silly loons
    Wha sent young Jemmy far frae me;
How dreary now are a' the towns,
    Where shepherds pip'd sae merrily :

How waefu' now upo' the plain,
Where younkers danc'd wi' hearts right fain;
For now ilk lassie mourns her swain,
    And sighs for him that's o'er the sea.

When last we met, ah, luckless morn!
    'Twas underneath the greenwood tree;
But soon he frae my arms was torn,
    Just as he vow'd to marry me:
Yet, when the cruel wars are o'er,
And shepherds hail their native shore,
I hope to meet, and part no more,
    Wi' bonny Jem that's o'er the sea.

SONG XXI.

KATE.

'STRANGER, if gentle pity swells thy breast,
' Let Kate thy pity move—ah! well-a-day!
' And turn not from a wand'rer sore opprest,
' Sighing for her love, slain far away.'

' Who was thy love, O fair but hapless maid,
' For whom I see thee weep?—ah! well-a-day!
' And why at eve mourn'st thou in this cold shade,
' For him who sound doth sleep far away?'

' Around yon cottage long young Henry toil'd;
' I heard his vows of truth—ah! well-a-day!
' Around yon cottage Peace and Pleasure smil'd,
' And maidens lov'd the youth, slain far away.'

z

' Let Hope, sweet maid! that cheers the path of all,
 ' To thee her comfort give—ah! well-a-day!
' Still some are doom'd to stand, tho' thousands fall,
 ' And Henry yet may live, far, far away.'

' Ah, no! by war forc'd from his promis'd bride,
 ' 'Twas here he sigh'd adieu—ah! well-a-day!
' And soon the tidings came, that Henry died,
 ' To love and honour true, far, far away.'

' To love and honour true!—a friend behold!
 ' Death only shall us part—ah! well-a-day!
' For thee I fought and bled, brav'd heat and cold—
 ' Still constant was this heart, tho' far away.'

' Art thou my love?—it must not, cannot be!
 ' My Henry once so fair!—ah! well-a-day!'
Pale turn'd her cheek—to earth's cold lap sunk she—
Now Henry in despair mourns far away.

SONG XXII.

ABSENCE.

HOW tedious, alas ! are the hours,
  The valleys no longer look gay ;
The meadows bespangl'd with flow'rs,
  No charms have when thou art away.
The villagers meet on the plain,
  At eve their gay pastime I see ;
But it only awakens my pain,
  Since I am far distant from thee.

Gay Summer the meads may perfume,
  And call forth the nightingale's voice ;
May cause each wild flow'ret to bloom,
  And bid smiling Nature rejoice :
Gay Summer would last all the year,
  If thou wert still smiling on me,
And a desert would pleasing appear—
  But, ah ! I am distant from thee,

In vain do I languish and pine,
　　Thy name is the theme of my song;
No pleasure, alas! now is mine,
　　But to think of thee all the day long.
O quickly thy presence restore,
　　That form which is dearest to me,
Or soon will my troubles be o'er,
　　For 'tis death to be distant from thee!

SONG XXIII.

ELLEN AND I.

SET TO MUSIC BY MR. HOOK,

And sung by Mr. DIGNUM, at VAUXHALL, 1794.

IN Spring, when sweet cowslips adorn the green vale,
　　And the lark's early melody wakes the fresh morn;
When the ploughman toils hard o'er the hill and the dale,
　　Or joins in the chase at the sound of the horn;
Then, wearied with labour, to Ellen I fly,
And few are so happy as Ellen and I.

In Summer, when nymphs to the meadows repair,

And trip round the hay-rick all joyous and gay ;

When each swain whispers soft a love tale to his fair,

And mirth, love, and innocence crown the long day;

Then at noon to the shade with fair Ellen I fly,

And few are so happy as Ellen and I.

In Autumn, when plenty enlivens the scene,

And round the pil'd sheaves see the reapers all roam;

When the younkers at eve gather round on the green,

To join the fond dance and proclaim harvest home ;

Then oft in the throng her sweet form I espy,

And few are so happy as Ellen and I.

In Winter, when Boreas blows keen thro' the vale,

And wither'd and leafless the trees all appear ;

When round the warm hearth flies the song, jest, or tale,

To beguile the long nights in this season severe ;

Then to Ellen's snug cottage transported I fly,

And few are so happy as Ellen and I.

SONG XXIV.

AUTUMN.

THO' the garlands are faded which Summer had
   wove,
   And the woods, hills, and meadows no longer look
   gay;
Tho' the blackbird's soft note steals no more thro'
   the grove,
   Nor the lark hails enraptur'd the brightness of day;
Tho' no more with coy Health by the streamlets I
   range;
Yet, blest with my Ella, I mourn not the change.

Her cheeks can the roses and lilies outvie,
   And all the wild flow'rets that wanton'd in June;
Her voice shall the voice of each minstrel supply;
   For oft in fond raptures, o'ercome by the tune,
I fancy 'tis spring, and the nightingale's near;
Or summer I view in the smiles of my dear.

Then sear, sickly Autumn! what Spring bade to bloom:
  Tho' on Winter loud calling, I heed not your rage,
While the smiles of my Ella dispel every gloom;
  For with her 'twould seem spring in the winter of age,
Who, guided by Virtue, a charm can impart,
Unknown to gay Splendour, Ambition, or Art.

SONG XXV.

JULIA.

OFT had I heard fond tales of love,
  But dreamt not nymphs would prove unkind;
I met fair JULIA in the grove,
  And hop'd with Love some sport to find.

Ye roses that adorn her cheek,
  Why thus your brightest bloom display?
Why thus a lover's ruin seek?—
  Alas! ye bloom but to betray.

I did but gaze, yet was undone ;
  For soon I own'd his painful smart,
And felt, too late, a smile had won
  What ne'er could have been gain'd by art.

So flies the linnet to the snare,
  The tempting bait in hopes to gain ;
But finds too late, for all his care,
  He struggles to be free in vain.

SONG XXVI.

TO-MORROW.

TO-MORROW's a cheat, let's be merry to day,
And to Time fill a goblet—'twill force him to stay.
Who but cowards would e'er at his summons repine ;
Who but cowards would steal from a liquor divine ;
For 'tis wine that can blunt the keen thorn of pale Sorrow,
As it moistens the flow'r that may fade ere to-morrow.

Since rosy Contentment dwells not with the great,

Leave wealth and dull thinking to slaves of the state;

But let Mirth and Good-humour our banquet still share,

And wine be our armour against sullen Care;

For 'tis wine, gen'rous wine, blunts the thorn of pale
 Sorrow,

As it moistens the flow'r that may fade ere to-morrow.

To-morrow's a cheat—the blest moments let's prize,

The sting of Reflection Age bids us despise.

Come, Friendship, then sweeten the care-drowning
 bowl,

That's sacred to Love, the delight of the soul;

For 'tis wine that can blunt the keen thorn of pale Sorrow,

As it moistens the flow'r that may fade ere to-morrow.

SONG XXVII.

NANNY OF THE TWEED.

How sweet to view the op'ning dawn,
When Phœbus ushers in the morn;
· How sweet to trace the flow'ry lawn,
When blossoms deck the spangl'd thorn:
The birds sing sweet o'er hill and grove,
And sweet's the shepherd's oaten reed;
But sweeter far the maid I love,
Fair Nanny of the Tweed.

· Let heroes fly in quest of fame,
And dauntless brave the battle's roar;
Let statesmen court a gilded name,
And sailors roam from shore to shore:
Dearer to me the hill and grove,
The rural dance and oaten reed,
When wand'ring with the maid I love,
Fair Nanny of the Tweed.

What tho' I'm doom'd, alas! by **Fate**
To tend each day my fleecy care,
Content would crown my lowly state,
* If she'd consent my flock to share :
Then blithe I'd sing o'er hill and grove,
And tune with glee my oaten reed ;
My days I'd pass in peace and love,
With Nanny of the Tweed.

SONG XXVIII.
DONALD.

I TOSS and tumble a' the night,
Fu' laith to lie my lane, lassie ;
Lang or the morn I wish for light,
For sleep I can get nane, lassie :
And aye this wee bit flutt'ring heart
It pants, and a' for thee, lassie ;
Love likes to act a tyrant's part,
And winna let me be, lassie.

By Labour wak'd at peep o' day,
  I greet alang the grove, lassie;
At eve I seek the birky brae,
  Fu' fain to meet my love, lassie;
    For aye this wee bit flutt'ring heart, &c.

I mark the wild flow'rs as they bloom,
  No half sae fair as thee, lassie;
The mournfu' mavis 'mang the broom,
  No half sae sad as me, lassie;
    For aye this wee bit flutt'ring heart, &c.

Let Fashion's fools, wi' gowd and land,
  In costly splendour shine, lassie;
Tho' I nae acres can command,
  An honest heart is mine, lassie:
    But aye this wee bit flutt'ring heart, &c.

Then haste to thy ain Donald's arms,
  And wi' his winsome bride, lassie,

This life will ha'e a thousand charms,
 Unknown to scornfu' Pride, lassie :
Syne ease this wee bit flutt'ring heart,
 It pants, and a' for thee, lassie ;
Love likes to act a tyrant's part,
 And winna let me be, lassie.

SONG XXIX.

WILLY OF EDEN SIDE.

NO younker on the village green
 Wi' my sweet Willy can compare ;
His rosy cheeks, and jet-black een,
 Mak' him the pride o' dance or fair.
In vain the lasses try each art,
 To lure the youth wi' gaudy pride ;
In vain they try to win the heart
 Of bonny Willy, smiling Willy,
Winsome Willy of Eden side.

Whene're the 'squire comes to our cot,
  He jokes and ca's me blythsome Kate;
But, lake-a-day! I lo'e him not,
  For a' his riches, pride, and state.
My aunty cries, ' Dear lassie, mind,
  ' And soon you'll be the 'squire's bride;'
But sweet content I ne'er can find
  Except wi' Willy, smiling Willy,
  Winsome Willy of Eden side.

How pleas'd am I at eve to see
  My bonny boy come o'er the hill;
He pous the sweetest flow'rs for me,
  And tunes his pipe so loud and shrill.
Whene'er he likes to kirk I'll gae,
  And wed wi' him, whate'er betide;
Then blythe I'll pass the live-lang day
  Wi' bonny Willy, smiling Willy,
  Winsome Willy of Eden side.

SONG XXX.

THE LOVELY BROWN MAID.

-◄··◄⊜►··►-

SET TO MUSIC BY MR. HOOK,

And sung by Mr. TAYLOR, at VAUXHALL, 1794.

WHEN May-scented zephyrs breathe gladness
　　around,
　Enliv'ning the meadow and grove,
And in each mossy cottage Contentment is found,
　Crown'd with health, peace, retirement, and love;
When far from the village the swains they retire,
　At noon to the lonely sweet shade ;
Grant me Health, rosy Health, all I ask and desire,
　With a smile from my lovely brown maid.

When my flocks bleat around me upon the wide plain,
　Contented I lie at my ease ;
And at eve I retire, free from sorrow and pain,
　To enjoy the soft fragrant breeze :

When music and gladness are heard thro' the grove,
  By moonlight I steal from the shade,
And o'er hills and deep valleys unheeded I rove,
  For a smile from my lovely brown maid.

Each morn I rise happy, each night I lie down
  With a heart free from envy and care;
In my plain humble cottage, far from the gay town,
  With my neighbours each comfort I share:
I envy no monarch, I boast not of wealth,
  No troubles my cot e'er invade:
All the blessings I ask is the blessing of health,
  And a smile from my lovely brown maid.

SONG XXXI.

KATE OF DOVER.

SET TO MUSIC BY MR. HOOK,

And sung by Mr. DIGNUM, at VAUXHALL, 1795.

NED Flint was lov'd by all the ship,
 Was tender-hearted, bold, and true ;
Cou'd work his way, or drink his flip,
 With e'er a seaman in the crew.
Tho' Ned had fac'd his country's foe,
 And twice had sail'd the wide world over,
Had seen his messmates oft laid low,
 Yet would he sigh for Kate of Dover.

Fair was the morn, when, on the shore,
 He flew to take of Kate his leave :
' My dear,' he cried, ' thy grief give o'er,
 ' For Ned will ne'er his Kate deceive ;

B B

' Let Fortune smile or let her frown,

  ' To thee I ne'er will prove a rover;

' All dangers in the bowl I'll drown,

  ' And toast my love, fair Kate of Dover.'

The tow'ring cliffs they bade adieu,

  To brave all dangers on the main,

When, lo! a sail appear'd in view,

  And Ned with many a friend was slain.

Thus Death, who lays the hero low,

  Robb'd Kitty of a faithful lover:

The tars oft tell the tale of woe,

  And heave a sigh for Kate of Dover.

SONG XXXII

SUMMER.

NOW the meadow, vale, and grove
Echo nought but songs of love ;
Health around her fragrance pours,
Flora decks her fav'rite bow'rs.

Nature, smiling, seems to say,
' In thy summer, man, be gay,
' Ere from thee coy Health is fled,
' And life's autumn bends thy head.'

Why then, Love, my thoughts control ?
Let me quaff the flowing bowl,
Till I banish hence dull Care,
And forget that JULIA's fair,

SONG XXXIII.

THE SWEETEST FLOWER OF YARROW.

SET TO MUSIC BY MR. HOOK,

And sung by Mrs. MOUNTAIN, at VAUXHALL, 1794.

SAY, have you seen my Sandy fair,
 Ye shepherds tell me true?
Last night he left me in despair,
 And, sighing, cried adieu.
O where can he stray, the bonny boy,
 Return my winsome marrow,
And fill this aching heart wi' joy,
 Thou sweetest flow'r of Yarrow.

Oft by pale moonlight thro' the mead
 We two did kindly stray;
Then sweetly on his oaten reed
 He pip'd so blythe and gay;

And oft beneath the shady tree
  He ca'd me his bonny marrow,
And vow'd he'd aye be true to me,
  The seewtest flow'r of Yarrow.

Adieu, ye nymphs and woodland swains,
  Each valley, dell, and grove,
Ye verdant meads and flow'ry plains,
  Where we were wont to rove:
This doleful tale some pensive maid
  May tell wi' mickle sorrow,
How Mary in the dust is laid,
  For the sweetest flow'r of Yarrow.

SONG XXXIV.

Go, winds, and whisper to my fair,
　　Adorn'd with ev'ry pleasing grace;
Tell her this bosom pants with care,
　　Since I beheld her beauteous face.

Go, bid the loves that on her wait
　　Steal softly from her snowy breast,
And bring from her a lover's fate,
　　That yet may make a lover blest.

Tell her I seek the lonely vale,
　　And carve her name on ev'ry tree;
That Echo hears my pensive tale,
　　But only laughs at love and me.

SONG XXXV.

HONEST JACK.

D'YE see, I'm a sailor that ne'er knew base fear;
It's true I'm a cripple—what then:
Tho' tight rigg'd fore and aft, and safe moor'd by
 my dear,
 Were I call'd on, I'd try them again.
Honest Jack is still happy and true to the end,
 Can drink, dance, work, laugh, joke, and sing:
I tipples my grog to my girl or my friend,
 And Jack's just as great as a king.

Now when poor Tom Hatchway was toss'd off the
 yard,
 Kit Fearful, the lubber, would cry:
' Avast there!' says I, ' tho' with Tom it's gone hard,
 ' Let's be thankful 'twas not you or I.'
  Honest Jack is still happy, &c.

Yer tempests and battles Jack minds not, d'ye see,

   Let winds whistle or loud cannons roar ;

The same Providence guards the poor sailor at sea,

   That keeps the land-lubber ashore.

     Honest Jack is still happy, &c.

When my fine larboard arm was shot off in the bay,

   D'ye think I'd palaver and sigh :

Says I to Sam Swig, when he hawl'd me away,

   '.There's Greenwich as dead as my eye.'

     Honest Jack is still happy, &c.

Tho' I've weather'd all storms, have oft stood at

   Death's door,

   And twice by false friends lost my all,

Yet I ne'er bore away from a messmate when poor,

   Nor e'er prov'd a shark to our Poll.

Honest Jack is still happy and true to the end,

   Can drink, dance, work, laugh, joke, or sing ?

I tipples my grog to my girl or my friend,

   And Jack's just as great as a king.

SONG XXXVI.

MY DEARY, O.

JUST where yon burn trots thro' the broom,
 Amang the birks sae mony, O,
Where gowans glint and blue-bells bloom,
 And lintwhites sing sae bonny, O,
A lass there lives right fair to see,
 Wi' gracefu' air enchanting, O,
Whase rose-bud cheek and sparkling e'e
 Ha'e set this heart a panting, O.
  Her presence mak's me cheery, O,
  Her absence mak's me weary, O :
   'Tis my delight,
   Baith day and night,
  To gaze upo' my deary, O.

I'd leave the town and a' its pride,
 The seat o' Vice and Slander, O,

c c

At eve yon burnie's flow'ry side
  Wi' my sweet lass to wander, O.
Let Fortune shun my lowly cot,
  And wealthy sauls frown on me, O,
The fickle jade I'd mind her not,
  Wou'd Annie smile upon me, O:
    Her presence mak's me cheery, O, &c.

Ye painted prudes, wi' a' your ait,
  In silk and siller flaunting, O,
Whase costly claise aft hides a heart
  Where modesty is wanting, O,
My Annie scorns your borrow'd grace,
  And, sweet as May-day morning, O,
Bright Health blooms on her cheerfu' face,
  In spite of a' your scorning, O.
    Her presence mak's me cheery, O,
    Her absence mak's me weary, O:
      'Tis my delight,
      Baith day and night,
    To gaze upo' my deary, O.

SONG XXXVII.

THE SEASON OF LOVE.

ELIZA, tho' thy charms appear
　　Like May when in her gayest dress;
Tho' sweet thy voice to my rapt ear,
　　And sweet the bloom that decks thy face;
That bloom, alas! must soon decay,
　　And Age thy charms will soon remove;
Then let us wisely, while we may,
　　Think youth's the season meant for love.

Behold, my fair, the smiles of Spring;
　　See how the fragrant hawthorn blows;
Hark! how the woods with echoes ring,
　　And view thine emblem in the rose:
But mark the change, when Winter drear
　　Spreads a white mantle o'er the grove;
Think, ere thou view'st the waning year,
　　That youth's the season meant for love.

Come then, Eliza, sweetest maid
　　That e'er inspir'd fond lover's song,
I'll lead thee to each fav'rite shade,
　　Where murm'ring Eden steals along.
In spite of cruel Fortune's frown,
　　Let us the joys of life improve ;
Nor blush, my fair, with me to own,
　　That youth's the season meant for love.

SONG XXXVIII.

COLLIN'S COMPLAINT.

Ｙ E shepherds, tell me, have you seen
Fair Emma of the village green ?
The roses deck her face so fair,
In tresses flows her auburn hair ;
The fairest of the fair is she—
But, ah ! she never thinks of me.

How oft beneath yon poplar's shade
I stole to see the village maid;
Now lonely thro' the vale I rove,
To shun Despair, and fly from Love.

With careless flight, the curious bee
From flow'r to flow'r still wanders free :
So I, ere Emma's face I knew,
From fair to fair contented flew ;
With village youths and maidens gay
I join'd the dance at close of day ;
· But now in vain I seek repose,.
And babbling Echo mocks my woes :
Then where shall hapless Collin rove,
To shun Despair, and fly from Love !

My flocks unheeded stray around,
My pipe hath lost its pleasing sound.
Ah, shepherds ! when she trips the plain,
Since you can witness Collin's pain,

Beware, fair Emma's beauty shun,
Or soon like me you'll be undone.
Ye faithful damsels see me laid
Beneath yon waving poplar's shade,
And pity Collin of the grove,
Who fell a prey to hapless love!

SONG XXXIX.
MUIRLAND WILLY.

SET TO MUSIC BY MR. HOOK,
And sung by Mrs. FRANKLIN, at VAUXHALL, 1794.

To yon lone cot out o'er the moor,
   That's shaded wi' green trees,
I aft steal frae my mither's door,
   Young Willy there to teaze;
Then sair she flytes at my return,
   And ca's me young and silly;
But, wae's my heart! I hate to mourn
   Sae near my Muirland Willy.

At bughting time, whene'er we meet
  In meadow, glen, or grove,
Wi' honey words and kisses sweet,
  He tells saft tales of love :
My cheeks he says are like a rose,
  My skin white as the lily,
My een are blacker far than sloes,
  The smiling Muirland Willy.

When at the market, dance, or fair,
  Bra' things he gi'es to me,
Baith pins and ribbands for my hair,
  Sae comely for to see ;
But when he wrestles on the green,
  I look baith saft and silly,
While tears run trickling frae my een,
  For fear o' Muirland Willy.

The youth is blythe, right fair to see,
  And free frae warldly pride ;

I ken fu' weel he doats on me,
  And means me for his bride.
When next we meet I'se tell my mind,
  And be no longer silly;
Then, if to marriage he's inclin'd,
  I'll wed wi' Muirland Willy.

SONG XL.

HENRY.

FAR on the main young Henry's sailing,
  Bending to his hard fate severe;
While his fond love, his loss bewailing,
  Mourns the sad absence of her dear.

For three long years a faithful lover,
  At last he nam'd the happy day;
When this his parents did discover,
  They forc'd my Henry far away.

What hopes and fears distract poor Nancy,
　To think of dangers he must brave ;
When winds are howling, oft I fancy
　He may have found a wat'ry grave.

Yon mossy bank I make my pillow,
　Where oft he own'd his tender flame ;
Or weep beneath the weeping willow,
　Where oft he carv'd his Nancy's name.

I view each well-remember'd token,
　The garters gay, ' Still constant be ;'
Or read upon the gold that's broken,
　' Remember Henry far at sea.'

Yes, Henry, yes, all offers scorning,
　Thy Nancy ne'er will faithless prove :
Can I forget the fatal morning,
　When last I parted from my love !

Cheer'd with the thought of thy returning,

   A while fond Hope dispels each care ;

But should Heaven change that hope to mourning,

   Thy Nancy soon will meet thee there.

SONG XLI.

DEARLY I LOVE JOHNNY, O.

SET TO MUSIC BY MR. HOOK,

And sung by Mrs. FRANKLIN, at VAUXHALL, 1795.

WHEN Sandy first a wooing came,

   He fondly try'd to win my heart,

And blush'd whene'er he own'd his flame;

   But soon I guess'd his wily art.

Tho' ilka lad in tartan plaid

   Should ca' me blythe and bonie, O,

They'd try in vain my heart to gain,

   So dearly I love Johnny, O.

Tho' Johnny canna boast of wealth,

  Contentment crowns his lowly state;

His ruddy cheeks denote sweet health,

  And goodness mak's the laddie great.

In Aberdeen sure ne'er was seen

  A youth sae blythe and bonie, O;

His flatt'ring tale can aye prevail,

  So dearly I love Johnny, O.

The ither morn upo' the bent

  I met my lad sae brisk and gay;

He vow'd, unless I'd gi'e consent,

  He'd o'er the hills and far away.

As hame we stray'd his pipes he play'd,

  And sang of love sae bonie, O,

I made a vow to buckle to,

  So dearly I love Johnny, O.

SONG LXII.

THE THRUSH.

THE sun had just withdrawn his beams
From silver Eden's winding streams;
The hind had wander'd home to rest;
Each feather'd minstrel sought his nest,
Save one, that, on a willow-tree,
A plaintive mourner seem'd—like me:
List'ning, methought I heard him say,
‘ I've lost my love—ah ! well-a-day !’

‘ Still to each other we prov'd true,
‘ No pair so joyous as we two ;
‘ We sung of LIBERTY so dear,
‘ And hail'd the beauties of the year ;
‘ At eve, beneath yon birchen shade,
‘ We charm'd the youth and artless maid :
‘ How chang'd, alas ! my former lay,
‘ I've lost my love—ah ! well-a-day.

' In spring, within yon briary glade,

' My love and I a nest we made :

' Soon tyrant man descry'd the place,

' And robb'd us of a tender race ;

' Since that this mortal foe I dread,

' By him I fear my charmer's dead :

' Thus left alone, I pine and say,

' I've lost my love—ah ! well-a-day !'

I listen'd to his plaintive strain,

And in my bosom felt a pain :

' Sweet THRUSH !' I cry'd, ' come live with me,

' Whose breast still harbours sympathy :

' Like thee—I once knew happier days ;

' Like thee—I sing my fair one's praise ;

' Like thee—in sadness I may say,

' I've lost my love—ah ! well-a-day !'

SONG XLIV.

THE PRESS-GANG,

SET TO MUSIC BY MR. HOOK,

And sung by Mrs. MOUNTAIN, at VAUXHALL, 1795.

ON Tay's sweet banks the lintwhite sings sae cheerily,
  Sweet blooms the violet and gowan in the grove;
The lambs o'er the meads they sport and play sae merrily,
  And the shepherd here at eve is fain to meet his love;
    'Twas here young Sandy first I knew,
    Sic youths as him they are but few,
    For he was comely, kind, and true;
      But, ah! one luckless day,
    A Press-gang forc'd my love to go
    To fight for them he never saw,
    And left me here quite sunk in woe,
      For Sandy far away.

On Tay's sweet banks they tore my laddie from me ;

O, sair did I weep when Sandy cried adieu !

In vain the shepherds try to heap their favours on me,

 In vain the lasses seek sweet flow'rs to busk my brow ;

  But shou'd the youth return again,

  'Twou'd ease this aching heart frae pain ;

  Then pleas'd I'd listen to his strain

   A' the live-lang day.

  My blessing aye attend my love,

  Mak' him your care ye pow'rs above,

  For weel I ken he'll constant prove,

   Young Sandy far away.

On Tay's sweet banks I us'd to sing sae blythe and gay,

 While Sandy pip'd so sweetly upon his oaten reed ;

Now lonely I wander, sighing sad, ah ! well-a-day!

 Nor heed the shepherds' dance at eve upo' the mead

  Whene'er we met upo' the plain,

  He ca'd me aye his Highland Jean,

  And prais'd my cheeks and sparkling een,

   Aye at close o' day.

When last we wander'd to Dundee,

He cried, sweet lass, I'll marry thee ;

But, O ! nae mair I hope to see

Young Sandy far away.

SONG XLV.

THE BEGGAR GIRL.

A POOR helpelss wand'rer, the wide world before me,

When the harsh din of war forc'd a parent to roam,

With no friend, save kind Heaven, to protect and

watch o'er me,

I a child of Affliction was robb'd of a home ;

And thus with a sigh I accosted each stranger—

' O, look with compassion on poor orphan Bess !

' Your mite may relieve her from each threat'ning

danger,

' And the soft tear of pity can soothe her distress.'

To the rich, by whom Virtue's too often neglected,
    I tell my sad story, and crave their relief;
But Wealth seldom feels for a wretch unprotected—
    'Tis Poverty only partakes of her grief.
Ah! little they think that the thousands they squander
    On the play-things of folly and fripp'ries of dress,
Would relieve the keen wants of the wretched who
        wander,
    While the soft tear of pity would soothe their distress!

Tho' bereft of each comfort, poor Bess will not languish;
    Since short is life's journey, 'tis vain to lament;
And he who still marks the deep sigh of keen anguish,
    Hath plac'd in this bosom the jewel content.
Then, ye wealthy to-day, think, ah! think, ere to-
        morrow
    The frowns of Misfortune upon you may press,
And turn not away from a poor orphan's sorrow,
    When the soft tear of pity can soothe her distress.

SONG XLVI.

THE PURSUIT OF HAPPINESS.

The poor hunt riches, and the rich hunt fame:
Vain mortals! happiness is but a name.

IN search of true Happiness vainly we wander,
   And each gew-gaw of pleasure with ardour pursue,
Till, by Fancy deluded, pert Folly turns pander,
   And we ne'er taste the joys that were first held to
      view.
With envy we gaze, as we onward keep pressing,
   At the trappings of State, or the mansions of Pride;
But that mortal on earth who enjoys life's pure blessing,
   Makes Content his companion and Virtue his guide.

How various the ways mankind take to gain greatness:
   With the miser 'tis greatness in riches to roll;
The beau thinks it lies in what fools term gay neatness;
   The drunkard still fancies it hid in the bowl:

Led on by false Hope, they right forward keep driving,
   Nor think how near Sorrow to Pleasure's allied ;
For in this world of folly but few are seen striving
   To harbour Content, or make Virtue their guide.

As insects from darkness round light fondly flutter,
   So mortals court Pleasure, and fall by the cheat ;
And when Age bids Reflection the plain truth to utter,
   'Tis then, only then, we behold the deceit.
But did man, helpless reptile ! ne'er aim at ambition,
   But seek lasting pleasures, and pity vain Pride,
Contentment would then act the part of Physician,
   And Virtue thro' life be his heart-cheering guide.

Epigrams, &c.

EPIGRAMS, &c.

EPITAPH

ON A WICKED MAN.

HERE lies what was a tool of Pow'r,
  Physician spite of Skill,
Who, if he knew not how to cure,
  He seldom fail'd to kill.

Ye honest men who wander here,
  Think ye have lost a foe :
Ye virgins, ye have nought to fear,
  Since Death has struck the blow.

Mourn drunkards, panders, gamesters, mourn,
  For you have lost the *knave :*
Ye bawds, with tears bedew this urn—
  Your friend lies in the grave.

DEATH AND THE DOCTOR.

So many had old Nostrum kill'd, that Death
At length grew jealous, and just stopp'd his breath.
A while thy labour now, grim king, give o'er—
Thou'st conquer'd him who kill'd full many a score.

TO WITLESS.

That Fortune's fickle I ne'er doubt;
  An' if she weel can see,
She maun be daft beyond dispute,
  To smile on ane like thee.

EPIGRAM.

' The proper study of mankind is man :'
Then tell me, men of learning, if you can,
Why is young Flippant call'd a brainless elf,
Who spends his time in gazing at himself?

THE IRISH ECHO.

SO civil's our Echo in Ireland, quoth Teague,
That, if you but whisper to't, how do ye do?
It answers, tho' distant far more than a league,
I'm very well, thank ye—pray, Pat, how are you?

THE HUSBAND TO DEATH.

THANKS, friendly Death, I now rejoice,
Her noise no more I fear;
Thunder was music to that voice,
Which yet methinks I hear.

TO AN *ARTIST*.

KNIGHT of the Brush, if thou wilt paint
Lords, lions, bears, and bishops still the same,
That strangers may know what is meant,
For heav'n's sake write below each creature's name.

F F

FORTUNE'S FOOL.

*P*OOR Tom last week was thought a dunce,
All wonder'd much at his thick sconce,
Who sat six hours, and spoke but once,
  And that indeed was deem'd great impudence.
Rich Tom, this week, all ask his hand,
Dogs, horses, men, doth Tom command;
He talks what none can understand;
  Yet all admire this murderer of sense.
Then why will man dame Fortune e'er despise,
Whose gifts oft make the greatest fool seem wise?

THE MISER'S FEAST.

W HEN Skinflint once a week doth dine,
  Bread serves for pyes, tarts, beef, and mutton;
Water he calls ale, beer, or wine;
  Then thinks himself expensive glutton.

EPITAPH.

HERE lies a wretch, to whom, we're told,
No pleasure life did give,
Who, when she could no longer scold,
No longer wish'd to live.

EPITAPH ON A FRIEND.

A Husband, parent fond, a friend sincere,
To Vice a foe, to Virtue ever dear;
One who well knew the world, and lov'd mankind,
Who liv'd in peace, belov'd, and died resign'd :
In wisdom old, ere he had reach'd his prime,
Death clos'd a life scarce sullied by a crime.
Such was the son of Worth who here doth lie—
Reader, like him, prepare in time to die.

THE END.

ERRATA.

Page vi, (preface), last line, for truts, read trusts.

—— 32, for Fragmemt, read Fragment.

—— 61, last line but one, for srife, read strife.

—— 72, line 4, for wale, read wail.

—— 97, — 9, for dimsome, read dinsome.

—— 115, — 5, for doth, read do.

—— 124, — 4, for concerts, read concert's.

—— 129, (motto), for Lorenza, read Lorenzo.

—— 140, line 6, for sweetness, read sweetners.

—— 177, — 8, read far, far away.

—— 197, — 4, for seewtest, read sweetest.